Praise for *The Last Detail*

"Goes right to the top of the tough-tender school of writing. Remarkably good . . . The writing is superb, the pace headlong, the irony tempered with a curious gentleness. How can anyone say the Novel is dead?"

—*Cosmopolitan*

"A salty, bawdy, hilarious, and very touching story."

—*Variety*

"Honest, heart-wrenching . . . a fine sense of pace . . . keeps his serio-comic escapade snowballing to the bitter end."

—*The New York Times*

"One of the ten best novels of the year."

—*Philadelphia Inquirer*

"One of the really excellent novels we will draw this year, and Ponicsán in his first appearance proves himself not only a master but a model of dialogue."

—*San Francisco Sunday Examiner and Chronicle*

"The first underground triumph of the '70s."

—*San Francisco Sun-Reporter*

"The characters are uneducated, tough, uncultured career sailors, but their warmth and affection come through, and readers become really involved with them—the innocent victims . . . of a heartless society. This book is sure to be a success."

—*Library Journal*

"A lean, funny, bitter book."

—*Boston Globe*

"A well-spun yarn that runs the gamut of emotions in anything but an ordinary story."

—*Fresno Bee*

"[An] excellent first novel . . . wonderful dialogue."

—*Publishers Weekly*

"So deeply human that the reader is apt to believe . . . that he is actually witnessing the events."

—*San Raphael Independent Journal*

"First novels tend to be flawed some place, but Darryl Ponicsán's is the exception."

—*Sacramento Bee*

"[A] gem of a first novel . . . face-paced . . . dialogue often is hilarious."

—*Fort Worth Star*

"An accomplished writer with a sure storyteller's touch."

—*St. Louis Post Dispatch*

"[An] exceptionally moving tale."

—*King Features*

"A polemic against military injustice and a testament to life, it is an exciting swiftly-paced piece of fiction whose mood shifts from uproarious comedy to frustrating tragedy."

—*The Sunday Star* (Washington, DC)

"Will make any serviceman say: 'Sure, that's the way it was.'"

—*Newsday*

The Last Detail

Also by Darryl Ponicsán

Goldengrove
Andoshen, Pa.
Cinderella Liberty
The Accomplice
Tom Mix Died for Your Sins
The Ringmaster
An Unmarried Man
Last Flag Flying

Under the name Anne Argula:
Homicide My Own
Walla Walla Suite (A Room with No View)
Krapps's Last Cassette
The Other Romanian

The Last Detail

A Novel

Darryl Ponicsán

With a New Preface by the Author

Skyhorse Publishing

First Skyhorse Edition 2017

First published in 1970 by The Dial Press. The first paperback edition was published in 1971 by The New American Library. An earlier version of the preface appeared in *The Stairway Press Collected Edition of* The Last Detail *and* Cinderella Liberty.

Visit our website at www.skyhorsepublishing.com.
Visit the author's website at darrylponicsan.com.

10 9 8 7 6 5 4 3 2 1

Library of Congress Cataloging-in-Publication Data

Names: Ponicsan, Darryl, author.
Title: The last detail : a novel / Darryl Ponicsan.
Description: First Skyhorse edition. | New York, NY : Skyhorse Publishing, 2017.
Identifiers: LCCN 2017015363| ISBN 9781510727755 (softcover : acid-free paper) | ISBN 9781510727779 (ebook)
Subjects: LCSH: United States. Navy—Petty officers—Fiction. | Naval offenses—United States--Fiction. | Prisoners—United States—Fiction. | Sailors—United States—Fiction. | GSAFD: Humorous fiction. | Road fiction.
Classification: LCC PS3566.O6 L37 2017 | DDC 813/.54—dc23 LC record available at https://lccn.loc.gov/2017015363

Cover design by Erin Seaward-Hiatt
Cover illustration courtesy of the Wright Press

Printed in the United States of America

To Dylan

Preface to the New Edition

CAME A DAY WHEN IT hurt to sit. I ignored the pain for a few days and when it didn't go away went down below to sick bay. My ship, the USS *Monrovia*, flagship of Amphibious Squadron 8 (the "Alligator Navy"), was tied to the pier in Norfolk, Virginia. We had recently returned from the Caribbean and were preparing to go on a Mediterranean deployment. A medical corpsman 2nd class ordered me to drop my dungarees and bend over. He peered and made his diagnosis: pilonidal cyst.

The corpsman sent me to the Portsmouth Naval Hospital for evaluation. The doctor there informed me that I did indeed have a pilonidal cyst which required surgery followed by thirty days' recuperation in the hospital. It seemed a bit excessive, but I tried not to question the ways of the navy.

The *Monrovia* was leaving in three days for a nine-month cruise. Apparently without me. Which made the surgery seem worth it; I was sick of sea duty and of that particular ship. In truth, I was sick of the US Navy. The military puts you in a place where all things are possible, and not in a good way.

I was admitted to the hospital on a Friday, with surgery scheduled for the following Tuesday. An entire ward was devoted to patients recovering from pilonidal cyst surgeries. Ambulatory patients swabbed the deck every morning then gathered in the day room at the end of the ward and played Monopoly. I joined them over the weekend, and each in his own way competed to find new ways to describe to me the horror and agony of what I was about to face.

Monday morning, we were called to attention at our bedsides and told to assume the position. Following the cue from the others, I hiked up my gown and bent over the bed. A doctor on his rounds trained his flashlight on the affected area. My cyst had miraculously disappeared! The doctor's medical opinion was that it had been a run-of-the-mill cyst that had run its course.

My ship had not yet cast off its lines, and I thought I might be able to catch it in time, but standard operating procedure mandated seven days to process and release a patient from the hospital. Again, don't try to question the ways of the navy. One of the oddest weeks of my service thus commenced, and of odd weeks, I did have a few. I was assigned to the hospital as temporary duty while being processed. My duties were to swab the deck and give assistance to any nurse who asked for it, though none ever did. I enjoyed liberty every day, from 1600 to 2400, known in the navy as Cinderella Liberty.

The chow at the hospital was so good that I would give up my first hour of liberty to eat there before I left to hit the sailor bars in Norfolk, which, besides a decent public library, are all I remember of that city. At 23:45 I would take a taxi back to the hospital, stagger to my ward, and fall into bed.

I had no friends and didn't care to make any during my week in limbo. I had no connection with my station, I was lonely, and my cash was running out. I fantasized what would happen if they lost my records and I became stuck in the hospital. There was precedent for lost records. In fact, it was a common fear among GIs.

During my time in the navy I wrote short stories and poetry. I had staked out a secret spot in the mimeograph room aboard ship where I would spend what little free time I had writing. My first paid story was published in a small quarterly, *Trace*, while I was still in the navy. I cashed the $25 check in San Juan, Puerto Rico, and spent it all that day on vodka gimlets at Trader Vic's. So one would assume my time in the hospital was worth writing about, and it was, but that's another story (my novel *Cinderella Liberty*).

Released from the hospital, I spent another week in limbo in the transient barracks. After my previous week of dissipation, I got back into shape playing pickup basketball games. I was awakened one night by a messenger telling me to get my shit together: I was going back to the *Monrovia*. No matter how dysfunctional, she was the closest thing I had to a home, so this was welcome news. At the time, I had no idea it would take more than two months to get back to her.

I reported to the USS *Intrepid*, now a floating museum in New York. Once again, I was on temporary duty, this time at sea. I was made the "assistant to the career guidance counselor." The career guidance counselor did not need an assistant; in fact, the

USS *Intrepid* did not need a career guidance counselor. The office was about four by six feet, hardly big enough for the two of us and a desk. The counselor was a crusty old first class who would never see another promotion. He was charitably kept in service until he could retire. A big, loud, and amiable sailor, he loved to play chess, which is what we did, endlessly. (We played for two months, and he beat me consistently. When I finally beat him, he gave up the game. Later, the same thing would happen to me. I played a shipmate for months, beating him all the time, until he beat me and I never played again. I have no explanation.) Aboard the *Intrepid*, I recall only two times when a sailor found his way to our office and wanted to discuss reenlistment. On both occasions, we urged the man to do it.

During those long empty hours as we played chess, the counselor and I swapped sea stories.

I told him mostly of my misadventures in transient duty, and he in turn told me of his own temporary duty as a prisoner escort, a "chaser" in navy parlance. He and another seasoned sailor were ordered to take an eighteen-year-old seaman apprentice from Corpus Christi, Texas, to the navy brig at Portsmouth, New Hampshire. The kid had been court-martialed for stealing a polio contribution box at the Navy Exchange and sentenced to twelve years. It happens. Or at least it did then. Draconian sentences for relatively minor offenses were not unheard of.

Unique among the armed services, the navy draws its cops from its own ranks as duty details. Any petty officer on any given night can find himself walking a beat as a Shore Patrol. The problem, or benefit, depending upon your point of view, is that the sailor carrying the gun or the club runs the risk of carrying his own humanity as well.

It was a long trip by train. Neither of the chasers or the prisoner knew each other, but they had time to become well-acquainted. The two escorts found themselves uncharacteristically sorry for the prisoner they had to take to the infamous brig run by Marines, for whom sailors have no affection, and vice versa. Their hearts told them to do something for him, short of helping him escape to Canada. The train was scheduled to pass through the kid's hometown, so they broke SOP and got off the train there, allowing the prisoner to visit with and say good-bye to his mom. But that didn't go well.

Rather than cut their emotional losses, they decided to try something else. They discovered that the kid was a virgin, and would remain so at least for the next twelve years. Unless they could get him laid.

I listened to the old salt talk about the detail, at times fall-off-the-seat funny, at other times hopelessly sad. My writer's radar pinged. The story was perfect. A messed-up kid who didn't want to be trouble for anybody, put into the hands of two lifers torn between a keen sense of duty and a mission they knew was wrong, between mild contempt for the kid and a begrudging affection. As soon as I could find a place and some moments to be alone, I started writing it down.

I worked on it as much as I could during the rest of my time on the *Intrepid*, which included liberty stops and debauchery in Palma de Majorca, Barcelona, Sicily, and a few more places that have thankfully faded from memory. I was put off the ship in Naples, pretty much worn out, and assigned to the naval station there, once more a transient. At night, I would go to the Piazza del Plebiscito, sit at a table outside, and order a bottle of red wine and several glasses. I would host a variety of prostitutes at my table. One after the other would take a break, have a glass of wine with me and gripe in broken English before getting back to work. I lived like that for a few weeks until, middle of the night, another messenger woke me up and told me to pack my sea bag. He gave me an envelope containing my records and orders and walked me to a duty carryall, which dropped me off at a deserted intersection in Naples. The driver told me to wait there. I watched the carryall drive away. It was 0400 hours, and I was alone in the Naples night, in a bright white uniform.

At the first light of dawn another carryall pulled up and I got inside. I was driven to an airstrip where I boarded a small navy plane. I had flown only three times in my life at that point, and never facing backwards. Wherever we were going, we took a detour to fly low over the water, looking for survivors from some incident I knew nothing about. Finally, we landed somewhere in Turkey. I sat for a few hours in a small room in a cinder-block structure watching Turkish TV until the civilian in charge told me to get on the helicopter.

It was a small Marine chopper with a crew of two who fretted over whether we would be able to get off the ground, for good reason. They had filled the cargo space with Turkish carpets and copper pots. No one told them they would have to pick up 180 pounds of sailor. The little chopper did indeed struggle to get airborne. I looked down, and not all that far down, over the craggy tops of mountainous terrain, realizing there was no place to land if we had to and hoping that if necessary to lighten the load the two Marines would throw out a carpet or two instead of me.

We made it over the mountains and out to sea. I was relieved when we landed on their mothership. I thanked them for the hop and was immediately ordered to crawl over the side of the ship, using the hanging cargo net, to the bobbing boat below. When I reached the last of the net I threw my sea bag onto the boat and waited for the right moment to leap. The two-man boat crew harangued me and mocked my manhood. I jumped and broke my fall on one of them. After ten minutes of skimming the sea I recognized the *Monrovia*. Home again.

I worked on the short story in the mimeograph room for the rest of my time in the navy, then put it aside to finish my thesis for a master's at Cornell. Later, I took it with me to Los Angeles and worked on it during summers while I was teaching high school English.

I am a veteran of the war in Vietnam, according to the motorcycle club that not long ago took me in, but I had been with the Sixth Fleet and never fired a shot in anger during that war. I was hardly aware of the war until I became a student again at Cornell, when it became hard to turn your awareness to anything else. In Los Angeles I became part of the antiwar protest. Though it is not a theme in *The Last Detail*, the Vietnam war is on every page.

In the summer of 1969, I took a creative writing course at Cal State Los Angeles with a novelist named Wirt Williams, a former naval officer. I had taken several writing courses in the past, first at Muhlenberg, then at the graduate level at Cornell, but Williams did not run his course like the others, in which students read aloud their work for group criticism. He thought that was just another way for writers to offer false praise or unwarranted condemnation. His method was to do a series of nuts-and-bolts exercises to be discussed one-on-one with him.

The first class exercise was to move like a camera from point A to point B, describing everything along the way. I rewrote from memory the opening of *The Last Detail*, a description of the transient barracks in Norfolk. When I sat down with Williams to discuss it, he asked, "Is there more of this?"

I showed him what I had, and he sent it on to his agent, Ned Brown, who called me and said he would like to represent me when I finished the novel. I didn't even know then if it was a novel. I had only the weekends to work on it, but those were marathon weekends. In October of that year, Brown called to tell me he had sold the book to Dial Press. In November, he called to say he had sold the film rights to Columbia. In January of 1970, I quit my job teaching and became a full-time writer.

To this day, I do not know how Columbia got the book. My agent had not yet submitted it to any film companies. At that time, it was still an unedited manuscript. When I first met the producer, Gerald Ayres, who had just moved from the executive offices to independent production at Columbia, I asked him how he got the book. He told me he found it on a subway car in New York.

What followed was the heady process of watching my book become a film. In the beginning, I wanted to do the adaptation, though I had never given much thought to the difference between writing a novel and writing a screenplay, and had never even seen a screenplay. My agent wisely suggested I not pursue it. To do a screenplay now would distract me from ever writing another novel, he said. Fortunately, Ayres kept me closely involved with the process, and I loved every moment of it, though I had no idea it would go on for so long.

A budget of three million dollars was worked out. This was in 1970, and *The Last Detail* was planned as a major production from a major studio. Think about that. I often do.

Robert Towne signed on as screenwriter. All I knew of him was that he had a good reputation as a screenplay doctor and had worked uncredited on a few successful movies. He wrote a first draft that met with resistance from the studio. This, I later learned, is a common event for any script. Fear was and is the driving force in the executive offices of movie studios. To Towne's credit, he fought back and refused to make the changes demanded by the studio. The development process came to a stop.

Ayres gave me a copy of the script for my opinion. Reading it was an odd and unsettling experience. For instance, there was the title page: "The Last Detail by Robert Towne." That aside, I was pleased to see that my dialog comprised about 96 percent of what was said. I accepted certain cuts and character tweaks as part of the process. What bothered me most was the new ending, and I argued for the one in the book. (A few years later, after I had written a couple of scripts myself, I understood why the ending was changed. It was a smart thing to do. To explain the reasons would take too much time here.) Ayres asked me if I wanted to take a crack at the script, for two weeks at ten thousand dollars a week. I had just resigned from a teaching job that paid ten thousand for an entire year of far more dangerous work. I took the job. A bonus was that my work qualified me for membership in the Writers Guild of America and health care coverage. I've been a union man ever since. I rewrote parts of the script over an intense two weeks. Ayres and the studio thanked me for my efforts, but little of what I added made it to the film.

During the stalemate between the filmmakers and the studio, I enjoyed the casting combinations they ran by me. At one time, it was Steve McQueen and Bill Cosby, at another Burt Reynolds and Roscoe Lee Brown. Finally, it was decided: Jack Nicholson would play Billy Bad-Ass, opposite an up-and-coming black actor named Rupert Crosse. They were having trouble casting the kid.

The front runner was an unknown actor named John Travolta. I was invited to lunch with Ayres, Towne, Nicholson, and Crosse at The Source on Sunset Strip, one of the first wholly organic vegetarian restaurants in Los Angeles. The banter between Nicholson and Crosse, who were already friends, put me right into the pages of my own book. Shortly after that, I got a call from Ayres that they finally cast the part of the kid. Most of the best young actors of the time were up for the role, but Mike Nichols urged them to test one who wasn't on the list: Randy Quaid. It seemed an outlandish suggestion. To begin with, Randy was a foot taller than Nicholson. No one, however, was going to ignore a suggestion from Mike Nichols. They tested Quaid, and everything that seemed to work against him wound up working for him: his size, his awkwardness, his voice. That particular casting was a stroke of genius. Like Nicholson, Quaid would be nominated for an Oscar, and so would Robert Towne.

The studio finally accepted that the script was not going to change. This was during that small window, not the whole decade as often believed, when the studios admitted they didn't know how to create movies and maybe they should trust the talent that does. They still had a lot of misgivings about the language, but they hired Hal Ashby, a hot young director in touch with the counterculture, to helm the project. The navy and the US government, as expected, refused any cooperation, which meant shooting in Canada. The project was gaining momentum again. Until Rupert Crosse was diagnosed with terminal cancer.

It was devastating news. Despite his condition, Rupert still wanted to be in the picture, so everything was put on hold while he sought alternative treatment in Trinidad. He didn't make it. Otis Young replaced him, and shooting began.

While all of this was happening, I made my way back to my experience in the navy hospital. I did not plan on writing anything else about the navy—I did not want to be typecast—but much of the delay of getting *The Last Detail* to film was because of the language, and that bothered me. The book itself was criticized for its salty language. By today's standards all that seems quaint. I had defended the language by saying, correctly, that sailors are known to swear a lot. Still, I began imaging a sailor who could not abide swearing, stuck in a hospital, his records lost, and needing to reconstitute some kind of family.

Unlike *The Last Detail, Cinderella Liberty* moved on a fast track. It was bought in manuscript by 20th Century Fox. This time I was asked by the director, Mark Rydell, to write the screenplay, and I jumped on it. I worked on the script for nine months, twice the time it took me to write the novel. A Writers Guild strike finally forced me to type: *Fade Out*. James Caan was cast in the lead, opposite an unknown actress named Marsha Mason, who won the Golden Globe and was nominated for an Oscar.

In an unusual alignment of forces, both movies were released on the same Friday in 1973. For a few weeks, I was the hottest writer in town.

Thirty years passed, long enough for me to find my way back to obscurity. If you haven't had a movie released in ten years, people in the industry assume they missed your obit. My last movie featured Matt Damon and Ben Affleck when they still had their baby fat. I hadn't published any books since then either, except for an oddball four-novel mystery series under the name Anne Argula.

I had among my aging fans, however, Tom Wright, a former Paramount executive who, like me, had exiled himself to Seattle, where we met. Every time I ran into Tom he would act out lines from the film, and remind me that *The Last Detail* was one of the classic movies of Hollywood's Golden Age and there ought to be a sequel, these many years later.

When the US returned to another soul sucking quagmire, this time in Iraq, Tom wanted to know where Billy Bad-Ass, Mule, and Meadows might be and what they might be thinking about Bush and his war. I didn't care. Which is not to say I didn't care about the war. Bodies were coming back from Iraq under a news blackout said to protect the privacy of the families of the deceased. Nightly I would watch the silent scroll on TV of the names and ages of the casualties and sink down into myself. I wrecked a couple dinner parties by dwelling on the cynical cruelty of the war and the plight of the young men and women ordered to fight it, none of them related to the man who started it, a privileged man who never had to go to war himself.

Tom continued to bug me, and while I was saying no to him I was already trying to overcome the first hurdle to writing the sequel, a notion that required a little suspension of disbelief, but stranger things have happened. As I said, in the military all things are possible. (For three months, as an example, I was the only sailor in an all-but-forgotten Army depot manned by twelve soldiers in the boondocks of Ohio.) Having cleared the initial hurdle, I wondered, what could possibly reunite those three veterans? In no time, I was back with them, the three shipmates of my own youthful creation, now old like me, still torn between duty and justice. The result is *Last Flag Flying*, the film adaptation of which is due out any day now.

Rereading *The Last Detail* in preparation for this foreword I cringed over some passages and wished I could rewrite or cut them. On the other hand, I was impressed by the sure-handed daring of the rest. As a screenwriter, I've since learned the discipline and vocabulary of rewriting, of doing serious demolition and redrawing entire floor plans. As a new novelist, I put more trust in my initial impulses.

Now, I can't believe that I let some of those lines get past me, but past me they went and I am not going to look critically over the shoulder of my younger self.

Darryl Ponicsán, 2017

(A note on that accent mark, which did not appear in the original edition of *The Last Detail*: Several years ago I went to Budapest and connected with some of the Ponicsáns still there. It is an odd name even in Hungary, though not as often mispronounced there as here. In Hungary, it is "pawn-ah-CHON"; in America, "PAWN-ah-son." It is too late now to correct the pronunciation, but it is never too late to add an accent mark if you are lucky enough to discover you own one. As patriarch of the American clan—anyone you meet with the name is related to me—I ordered all Ponicsáns in America to use the accent. None of them did.)

The Last Detail

One

THE TRANSIENT BARRACKS AT NORFOLK Naval Base are deserted at nine this morning, or almost deserted; Billy Bad-Ass, First Class Signalman, is asleep in the TV room at the far end of the barracks. On the centerline is a row of lockers, half-lockers really, one atop the other. Each is secured by a lock, a combination lock for those who can't keep keys, a regular lock for those who can't remember combinations or who tend to come in drunk after taps. On each side of the lockers is a row of double metal bunks. All are neatly made, not with dressed blanket edges and not tight enough for bouncing the legendary quarter, but this is not boot camp. Some of the bunks are unused and the mattresses are rolled to one end, stained with urine, semen, sweat, spit, and Wildroot, and flattened by a generation of anonymous sailors. The springs underneath are flat strips of metal that have long since reached their tolerance and have never sprung back from it. Many sailors have met the morning unable to straighten their bodies and hardly able to draw breath because of them.

Just inside the door, a seaman apprentice rubs his hands together and does a quick little dance to circulate the blood. It was cold outside, but here in the transient barracks the heat is enough to nudge you. He opens his peacoat and walks across the newly buffed deck in a cocky swagger he uses when there's no one around who outranks him.

He, like the first class signalman in the TV room, is a transient, temporarily working as the master-at-arms' messenger. He is well-off in his cushy job where he can drink coffee and smoke cigarettes as much as he pleases. There is no explanation for why he has his job and why the messcook in the galley has his. Perhaps the third class yeoman who checked him into the base liked the ring of his name.

He knows where to find Billy, as does the MAA who sent him. Billy has that which inspires tolerance: time in and rate. What's more, he reads a lot of books, sometimes even reading the same one more than once.

Across the doorway that has no door is a chain. From the chain hangs a sign: SECURED. The messenger puts one chilly palm on the door frame and leans over the chain. He sees Billy, asleep on one of the tattered red leatherette sofas. He is in his dress blues, which means he was on the beach last night, which means anything, though in Billy's case surely not nothing. Three red hash marks slice diagonally down his forearm. Three hitches of four years each. And he is now on the fourth. His arm hangs over the side and the back of his hand, palm up, is on the deck next to his white hat. Next to that is a battered paperback copy of *The Stranger* by Albert Camus, and next to that is an upright, nearly empty bottle of Ripple. He snores in uneasy spurts.

The messenger steps over the chain. The cocky swagger is gone. He shakes Billy gently. "Bad-Ass, wake up, it's way the hell past reveille. You missed chow."

Billy stirs and rolls over onto his back. His eyes click open and he is awake, though still. There is no yawning and stretching. He has the tendency to open his eyes wider than is necessary and the forehead that was at ease in sleep becomes wrinkled. He looks older than his age, thirty-two.

"Did you say I missed chow?"

"Yeah, it's after nine."

"Tell me that's not why you woke me, lad. Would you tell me that?"

The messenger moves back uneasily. No one here has ever seen Billy in a violent moment, but no one suspects that he is nonviolent.

"No, man, the chief MAA sent me. He wants to see you right away."

"Well, did you tell the chief MAA that he could go fuck himself?"

The messenger smiles. "Yeah, but he said he ain't in the mood and I'd better get you fast or it's my ass."

"What can he do? Put you in the galley, up at four thirty, knock off at eight o'clock, good training for a young seaman deuce."

"C'mon, man, don't break my balls, I'm just trying to get along. It's something really big-deal I think. Maybe your orders came through."

"Maybe," says Billy Bad-Ass. "Maybe tomorrow I'll be in a new ship and underway to a new place where everything's different and they don't know me and I don't know them. You got a ciggy?"

The messenger gives him a cigarette and Billy puts one hand beneath his head and smokes.

"Fell asleep last night, you know where?"

"Yeah, here."

"No, before that. Fell asleep on the railroad tracks. Yeah. My head right on the rail. Like to freeze it off. Wonder what a man looks like when a train's gone over his frozen head. Something to think about."

"What were you doing?"

"I had just got it for free."

"No shit?"

"Yep, a radioman's old lady off the Rockridge. Didn't cost me a dime. Matterafact, she gave me this wine when I left. You're talking to a very big dealer."

"Back home I got it for free all the time, all I wanted."

"Everyone gets it back home. Get it in Norfolk, that's the challenge. But, lad, you're talking to the original Billy Bad-Ass. You ain't had pussy since pussy's had you. Your momma told me. And did you ever notice you look a lot like me? I think I knew your momma."

"Yeah, yeah, yeah,"

"C'mere a little closer, lad. I'm gonna make a confession to you."

The messenger is tentative. He doesn't trust Billy. He inclines his head toward him but not so close that he couldn't leap away if he had to.

"Sometimes," says Billy, "I think there's more to life than pussy. I tell you this only because you're a nice kid and I think you can keep a secret. Billy Bad-Ass says, sometimes there's more to life than pussy."

"Gee, Mr. Bad-Ass, can I put that on a plaque and hang it at the end of my rack when I go to sea?"

"They'd never send a shitbird like you to sea."

"Like hell. I know my orders are going to be for some damn tin can and I'm gonna wind up on the friggin' deck force."

"What's this navy coming to, trust a baby like you on deep water."

"Think I'm crazy about it? Remember what they say: the worst shore duty is better than the best sea duty."

"You been listening to a lot of noise from crusty old stew-burners who shouldn't be in the navy anyway. They should be frying onions in some slop chute. There ain't nothing better in the *world* than being on the sea—even in the navy. When I'm at sea, I'm up on the bridge talking to *ships,* man. Across miles of liquid real estate, I'm communicating with a ship. Okay, so it's only another signalman, but you know what I mean. There ain't no place where the air is cleaner and you might see flying fish or porpoise or even a whale if you luck out. At dusk the sky might be like it's on fire and in the morning it's as sharp as a crack across the face. And then you have storms where you have to lash yourself in the rack, but when it's over you rock to sleep like you were a baby again. So don't give me a ration of noise about shore duty. When you're out at sea, you're doing *man's* work and there ain't much of that left any more. Besides, you don't get into trouble at sea. No booze, no pussy, no money. Just a man and his job."

"Jesus, Bad-Ass, stop it, I'm getting all misty inside."

"I got your misty inside—dangling, lad."

The messenger pushes Billy's book with the toe of his shoe and asks, "What're you reading?"

"Book about a guy kills another guy."

"Anybody get laid in it?"

"No. Yeah. He does get laid in it."

"Any good?"

"Pretty good. This guy writes with a pencil."

"Huh? What do you mean, with a pencil?"

"Lotsa guys write with Dictaphones. You know, never use one line of dialogue when you can run it up to three pages, but this guy, this Camus guy. Something else."

"You oughta write skin books, Bad-Ass, you got a good line of shit. I like 'em where everybody gets laid and there's no wasting time on descriptions."

"No descriptions?" says Billy. "Not even like, 'My tongue seemed to have a mind of its own and slid up her smooth white thigh to the dark silken fleece of her Venus mound and then through to the warm moist shelter of her grotto of passion?'"

The messenger whistles softly through his teeth. "Jesus Christ, Bad-Ass! Where'd you learn that? You really oughta be writing skin books."

Billy sits upright. He finishes the Ripple in one long pull, replaces the top, and throws the empty into a nearby wastebasket. The loud noise it makes makes him press his temples for a moment. Then with his hands he signals to the messenger, who doesn't understand the semaphore: QUEBEC, UNIFORM, INDIA, ECHO, TANGO—quiet. Talking with his hands in semaphore is a habit he fell into when he was learning his trade. He would practice while waiting in the chow line, standing watch, sitting on the pot, so that now his hands move so rapidly over the signals they look like blue jays bothering a cat. He is hardly conscious of the habit.

He stands up, gives his white hat to the messenger, and puts the book under his armpit. With the messenger trailing him, he walks down the line of lockers, rapping random ones with his fist, making them clang in the stillness of the barracks.

"See here, lad. Sailors. Every locker a sailor. See this dent. An elbow. Here a knee, here a head. Every part of the human body has taken a whack at these lockers. Know what's inside?" He hits a locker. *"The New Testament!"* He hits another. "A French tickler." He continues to hit the lockers. "A tiki charm from St. Thomas, a flying cock-and-balls from Naples, a framed picture of a yellow-haired girl, a funny deck of playing cards."

He stops banging the lockers when he comes to his bunk. He tosses the book on the bunk, pulls off his towel and slings it around his neck.

"All of them together, they make a pretty good psychology textbook."

"What's in yours?" asks the messenger.

"Stephen Crane."

"Who's he?" asks the messenger.

"A skin book guy."

"Oh."

Billy takes his douche kit out of his locker and hooks it over his little finger. With the messenger trailing him, he walks unsteadily toward the head, semaphoring with his hands: HOTEL, ECHO, ALPHA, DELTA. They go into the head. Nine of ten urinals have masking tape across them and are marked: SECURED. Billy rips the tape away from one and fumbles with the thirteen buttons on the front of his trousers.

"You know, lad if I were a marine, I wouldn't have to mess with these buttons. I'd just take off my hat."

The messenger laughs. Billy tears the tape off a wash bin. He fills it up with water and plunges his head into it.

Billy's name, of course, is not Bad-Ass. In the same way that Pigalle became Pig Alley, that San Pablo became Sand Pebble, Buddusky became Bad-Ass, which in navy parlance means a very tough customer. The term is always used with the name Billy to achieve the effect of the alliterative trochee. If it were not his natural given name, his shipmates would have called him Billy anyway.

Billy does not feel one way or the other about the distortion of his surname. The truth was that Buddusky itself was a distortion of some other similar-sounding name. During the great immigration push Billy's grandfather, a twenty-year-old cabinetmaker, stood with the huddled masses on Ellis Island and gave his name to a civil service officer, who, a bit peeved by these absurd Polish names, wrote down what he thought he heard. Billy's grandfather thought only an ungrateful fool would question the way things are done in America; so from that moment on he became Buddusky and the other name, whatever it had been, was never used again.

His grandfather drifted out of New York after landing and supported himself by doing some intricate work on church organs in Pennsylvania. He spent three years in the Allentown-Easton-Bethlehem area and was known as a sober, promising young craftsman. In Allentown he met Mary Grace Prosick, a seamstress his age, and they decided that it would be a wise economic move to marry.

A friend told him that coal and the railroad were making the Scranton-Wilkes-Barre area a prosperous place in which to make a home. The Protestant churches in the Lehigh Valley had been good to Billy's grandfather but he thought he should not count on such luck continuing indefinitely. They moved to Scranton and settled in an area known as Providence, a homey, pleasant place built on small hills of cobblestone roads and inhabited by butchers, carpenters, miners, railroad men, and other assorted laborers and craftsmen. They were predominantly German, but there were strong enclaves of Russians, Lithuanians, and Poles.

It was in Scranton that Billy's grandfather attained his life's only distinction, the one thing he could, and did, talk about for the rest of his days: he worked for the Scranton family. In their mansion he built one corner cabinet and the family was so taken by his diligent craftsmanship and the beauty of his woodwork that they retained him for several months on a variety of projects. After that he could always say to business prospects, "I worked for the Scrantons and they liked my work." His family would never know poverty. To his friends he could describe the interior of the Scranton mansion and comment upon the personalities of its inhabitants. He often said that young Bill Scranton would be governor someday and it would have pleased him immeasurably to see it, but he died three years before that happy event.

Billy's father was born in Scranton, the first of four children. He was named Stashu and he carried the family's dream for a scholar. John, born eighteen months later, was to be his father's apprentice, but instead went into the mines until his first near-fatal cave-in. After that he headed west and was killed in Tulsa when a valve he was unloading from a freight car fell on him.

The two girls, Sophie and Ruth came next. Sophie died at seventeen when her mother gave her a physic for a stomachache that turned out to be appendicitis, and Ruth became an itinerant tramp whose aim in life was to wake up every morning in a different town next to a different man. Billy cannot remember ever seeing Aunt Ruth, and her name was seldom mentioned.

So it was for Stashu to fulfill his parents' dreams of having an educated man in the family because throughout the history of the Buddusky and Prosick families there had never been a man with a degree or diploma of any kind. When Stashu finally did receive an B.A. in English from Stroudsburg State Teachers College, the family fairly exploded with pride. For two days friends and neighbors came in to drink beer and eat kielbasa, pierogies, bleenies, and if anyone had said that Stroudsberg wasn't such a hot school anyway, Stashu's father could not be held responsible for what he might do. It was a *degree,* from an accredited four-year college, and Stashu was recognized on campus as being a very good student. What's more, he was to be a teacher in Andoshen, an anthracite town sixty miles southwest of Scranton. At last, an intellectual Buddusky. It could happen only in America. Stashu's father was content.

Stashu, however, was not. He too took great pride in his accomplishment, but it was not enough. Always there was in the back of his mind the voice that whispered, "Dumb Polack." He wanted to become principal of the school even before he began his first day there as a teacher.

He quickly established a reputation as an "ambitious young teacher." He volunteered for every committee and willingly accepted all assignments. He was well-liked by the rest of the faculty because they were not so ambitious and were glad to be relieved of onerous tasks.

But he never did become principal. He could never even make department chairman on the small faculty. At first he thought it was because he was Polish, but in Andoshen Poles and Lithuanians were in the majority. Then he thought it might be because he was trying too hard, so he relaxed. He stopped volunteering, he groused occasionally. He soon found he enjoyed relaxing and stopped pushing altogether. His popularity with the students, never high, improved somewhat, the esteem of his colleagues did not lessen and he never made department chairman or principal. He finally confessed to himself that he was nothing but a dumb Polack and he might as well lie back and enjoy it. He never bothered to find another job.

When he was thirty he married Ellen Berbow, an elementary school teacher, twenty-seven and a native of Andoshen. Three years later they had a son, William James and three years after that had another son, Ernest Scott.

In spite of his father's reputation as the family intellectual, Billy, at about age twelve, considered him something of a birdbrain and that early assessment of his father never changed with the passing years. He rejected his father's advice to attend Bloomsburg State Teachers College and instead joined the navy. His reason for joining the navy was that it was the only service whose uniform did not require you to wear a tie. He had no reason for joining the service in general except that he was told he could retire when he was thirty-eight, and since most people don't retire until sixty-five, the service sounded like a pretty good deal. Besides, he wanted to get far away from his father, who had a habit of spoiling things for him. Books, for instance. Billy started reading at an early age and enjoyed books until his father insisted that he understand them. Even though his father talked books to death, Billy didn't stop reading. He read on the sly instead and never spoke to his father about another book unless it was a schoolbook and he had no way out. The other books he would read and think about for himself. It took him years to be able to read a book and ignore the demands of his father. At eighteen Billy made a discovery that improved his relationship with his father. He discovered geography and put as much of it as he could between him and his family.

* * *

The messenger puts Billy's white hat on the basin next to him and looks in the mirror to adjust his own.

"See you, Bad-Ass. I got to run and find that spade they call Mule. Chief wants him too. Big-deal stuff."

The messenger leaves Billy with his head still submerged and searches the base, tracking down the sailor called Mule. Mule, a first-class gunner's mate, also inspires tolerance though he has no time for books. He has other interests and is harder than Billy to find, but the messenger knows his business and follows one lead after another until he finally steps inside the refrigerator in the salad room of the galley. Mule is on his knees, in dungarees, with half a dozen of the messcooks, shooting craps. They are all shivering from the cold. The messenger says, "Hey, Mulhall, the MAA wants to see you right away. Big deal."

Mule has a carrot in his mouth. He is rubbing the dice between his palms. He talks around the carrot, first to the dice, then to the messenger. "C'mon, baby, you got me the gas, now get me the Caddy. Did you tell the MAA to go to hell on a forklift?"

"Yeah I tell him all the time but he says to find you or it's my ass."

Mule throws the dice. A five and a three. There is a hubbub of, "Two says he'll eight . . . you're covered . . . three he won't . . . betting against the dice . . . you're faded." He throws. A six and a three.

"I ain't jiving," says the messenger. "He really wants you right away."

"Eighter from Decatur, eighter from Decatur."

He tosses the dice again and loses, a four and a three. He looks at the messenger. "You ain't exactly lady luck, are you, boy?"

"Look, man, give me a break. I'm just trying to get along. The man sent me to find you. Said it's very big-deal stuff. Maybe you got orders, I don't know."

Mule gathers his money, gets to his feet, and says to the others, "Gentlemen, there will be other days and other games. Don't spit in the salad."

When Mule rises to his feet, he pauses before walking in order to allow the achy feeling in his legs to pass. He wants no one to notice. Like Billy, he has fourteen years in and he can't give them any opportunity to give him the heave-ho before he puts in his twenty and gets a pension. He knows of others who have been forced out with only a couple of years to go. There was a lifer in San Diego who was dumped for indebtedness. The old man got sick of the dunning letters so he had the man discharged and thereby made the matter a non-navy problem. Another guy in Corpus Christi was on his nineteenth year when he made it with his girlfriend's jailbait daughter, who wanted to get at the old lady. The old lady blew the whistle on him and he was busted out.

They could probably nail him on a fraudulent enlistment since he had lied on the medical forms. If there had been a place for malnutrition under childhood ailments he *would* have checked that. All they had to eat was what grew wild in their corner of the world in Louisiana, and the occasional windfalls that grubbers for survival seem to turn up when fate is tightening its grip.

He remembers his father as a head-scratching, foot-shuffling odd-job boy who aspired to be a house nigger. Early in his life Mule thought of his father as a clever masker fooling the white folks as a matter of economic necessity. Then his father went away, leaving his woman with four unwanted children, a shack with rent in arrears, and a bag of rice. When he left there was not enough cash at home to buy a stick of gum. The last they heard was that he was in Tuscaloosa, Alabama, with an advanced case of syphilis. The family decided that was a good place for him to be.

Mule, whose actual name was Richard Mulhall until his shipmates renamed him, learned how to read and write well enough to join the navy, in his mind the military elite, where it was guaranteed that you'd never have to eat out of a helmet or sleep on the cold ground. The navy was Mule's salvation, a place where you could eat three gigantic meals a day and use the same facilities as anyone else.

Throughout his years in the navy he made sure that his family back home had enough to eat, too. Now that the two girls were married and out of the house, and his younger brother Earl was in one or another jail, his mother was making out all right on his allotment. She wouldn't have to rot somewhere under a pile of rags like so many of her contemporaries. As for Mule, his battle against malnutrition could never be ended. There were too many reminders—the aching in his legs, for instance, when he went from a kneeling to a standing position.

The messenger hurries out of the galley and back to the MAA's office. He has done his job, found and told them, and now he can sit on his stool and enjoy his coffee and a cigarette and listen to the sea stories. The MAA, a chief bosun, also drinks coffee as does his yeoman, who listens to him say, "When I was in the 'gator navy, you know, in the Med doing amphibious landings with the marines, I knew one of the commodore's yeomen who worked in the staff office. This guy used to keep the records and file the reports on everything that happened on the cruise, you know what I mean, the stuff you don't see on the op-orders, like how many marines beat up how many civilians during liberty at Palma Majorca and what was done to cover it up. You know.

"Well, one of the records he kept was the V.D. count. Listen, us guys are goddamn saints compared to the grunts. For every case we had, they had five or six. 'Course they throw 'em down in the hold there like rats and spiders for the whole cruise so how'd you expect them to act when they're let out—like rats and spiders? But once we did an off-load on this deserted island near Sardinia, someplace where there wasn't even a snake living. You know. The jar-heads were there for three days playing war. After they came back on board, come to find out that four of them had picked up the clap. Christ, if there's *something* to be screwed somewhere, the marines will find it."

The messenger joins in the laughter and can't wait until he will have such tales to tell.

"Which reminds me of a joke," says the chief. "It's World War Two and this guy is going overseas. He tells his old lady, 'Sweetheart, I'll be true to you,' and she says, 'Yeah, I'll bet.' So he goes to England and all his pals are getting some but he stays true to his wife, and he goes to Paris and all his pals are getting some, but he stays true to his wife. Finally he's at the front line and it's been almost a year. He's horny as he can be. He's there in the trenches and he sees this little pig running in front of him. He can't control himself anymore so he jumps up and screws the pig. You know. Then the war is over and he goes home to the old lady and says, 'Sweetheart, I was true to you.' And she says, are you ready for this, she says, 'In a pig's ass you were!' And he says, 'Goddamn those German spies!'"

The chief beats his desk with his open hand and laughs. The yeoman and messenger bounce in their chairs. After they calm down, the chief says, "You know, though, whenever I go on a long cruise my old lady says it's all right if I buy a piece of tail as long as I don't bring anything home and as long as there's none of that love stuff. She doesn't go for that."

Billy Bad-Ass has been leaning on the counter during the last half of the joke, looking at the huge muster board on the wall. He does not laugh at the bosun's story. He says, "Well, what's the skinny?"

The chief looks up from his coffee cup and says, "Buddusky, you're one lucky son-of-a-bitch. How come you always come up smellin' like a rose?"

" 'Cause I go down smellin' like a rose. Where am I going?"

Mule arrives and stands next to Billy at the counter. The chief says,

"Buddusky, meet Mulhall. You two guys will be working together. You're another lucky son-of-a-bitch, Mulhall."

Billy and Mule shake hands, and Mule says, "What's happening?"

"You two dudes pulled temporary duty as chasers."

"Where to?" asks Mule.

"Portsmouth Naval Prison." The chief busies himself with their orders.

Mule and Billy look at each other with big smiles. They are a couple of lucky sons-of-bitches. "Who're we taking?" asks Mule.

"A seaman, used to be, named Meadows, Lawrence. Drew eight years and a DD."

"What did he do, kill the old man?" asks Billy.

"C'mon inside here," says the chief.

They go inside the office and have a seat. The messenger jumps to and gets them each a cup of coffee.

"Who'd he kill?" asks Billy.

"Didn't kill nobody. Robbery," says the chief.

"What'd he hit?" asks Mule.

"The commissary store."

"On base here?"

"Yeah. Dumb ain't it?"

"His mother raised a fool, that's sure."

"Working a shit detail there. I assigned him myself, but I don't remember who he was," says the chief.

"How much did he lift?" asks Billy.

"Forty dollars," says the chief.

"You're shitting me," says Mule.

"I wouldn't shit you. You're my favorite turd," says the chief.

"Eight years and a DD for forty bucks? I thought they only pulled that in the army."

"Yeah, well, don't kid yourself. They caught the kid red-handed."

"Don't it sound like somebody's fucking over Meadows?" says Mule.

"Well told," says the chief. "The thing is, he tried to lift a polio contribution box. You know."

"Oh, man, a weirdo. Does he wet the bed too?"

"Well, he sure picked the wrong thing to lift. The polio boxes are the old man's old lady's personal do-gooder project. She's responsible for the polio contributions on base and every year they make a fuss over her and give her a plaque or something, you know, for collecting a bundle for charity. Then along comes this Meadows shitbird and fucks charity. It ain't the kind of thing the old man's gonna take kindly to, right?"

"But Jesus, eight years."

"And a DD."

"I did eight days in the brig once," says the chief MAA.

"Some fun, huh?" says Billy.

"Yeah, but long termers, you know, it's not like the brig. They take it easier on long termers. Christ, I was on piss 'n punk for three of the eight days."

"What's piss 'n punk?" asks the messenger.

"Bread 'n water," Billy tells him. "They don't do that much anymore, though. Guess they're getting soft."

"Yeah, first it was wooden ships and iron men and now it's the opposite—and all that bull," says Mule.

"Well, at least it's good duty for you guys. I'd trade places with you."

"Yeah, we're a couple of lucky son-of-a-bitches," says Billy.

Two

THEY LEAVE THE MAA's OFFICE together and return separately, each carrying his AWOL bag. An immaculate sailor is a beautiful sight that is by no means accidental. An immaculate sailor spit-polishes his shoes for hours until they capture and hold the light. He wraps masking tape around his hand and pats the trousers and jumper of his dress blues until they are totally free of lint. He presses his own uniform with a steam iron and a damp cloth to make sure the reverse creases running down the sides of his legs and arms are straight and definite. When he takes the uniform off he folds it in an elaborate inside-out pattern in order to maintain the creases. He takes a toothbrush and scrubs the white piping of his jumper until it gleams. He rolls his neckerchief until it's as round and firm as a rope. He works his white hat until the brim rolls over evenly all around the top, then keeps it in a clear plastic bag. The white hat is the most important article of his uniform. It must be placed with great care exactly two fingers above the very top of the nose so that it rests just above the eyebrow line. If a sailor is to be beautiful, the white hat must be perfect in all respects. This done, he stands with his back slightly arched so that there is a suggestion of a pouch between the legs, his hands hanging limp as though ready to draw for a gun. This picture of the immaculate sailor has recruited more young men than all the pamphlets describing the opportunities and benefits the navy has to offer.

Billy and Mule stand in the MAA's office, two immaculate sailors. Larry Meadows slumps in a chair in the corner of the office. He is not an immaculate sailor. He could never recruit others. He sits as if trying to disappear inside his peacoat. His jumper flap is bunched up against the collar of his peacoat. He wears stainless-steel handcuffs and holds his dingy white hat listlessly with both hands. His shoes are only brushed. He does not look up from them, nor does he move, yet he seems to slip deeper into his peacoat.

The messenger stands in another corner, his back against the wall, frightened for no reason except that Meadows is eighteen, his own age. He does not jump to get anyone coffee. He pulls at a rough cuticle.

The yeoman is all business and goes about pulling copies of orders, stuffing them into envelopes and checking travel vouchers and meal tickets with cool mechanical efficiency. When he finishes he takes off his glasses and puts them into his jumper pocket. He hands the pile of paperwork to the chief MAA and leans back in his chair, folding his arms across his chest.

"Okay, Buddusky," says the chief, "you're the honcho. Here's Meadows' stuff." He hands Billy a large manila envelope sealed with tape. He hands Billy and Mule two unsealed white envelopes. "And here's your orders, travel chits, and meal tickets."

Billy and Mule put them into their inside peacoat pockets. "The carryall and driver are outside to take you to the bus. You take the bus to Richmond and the train to Washington. Then up to New York and Boston and you get another bus to Portsmouth. It says on the orders that you're to arrive no later than twenty-four hundred on nine February. That don't mean you should play grab-ass for five days before showing up at Portsmouth. You get your asses up there just as soon as you can. If you take one day more on the return trip than on the going trip, well, that's understandable. Here's the keys to the cuffs. Each of you gets one key."

The chief opens his desk drawer and takes out two .45's with holsters and guard belts. On top of each is a form. "Both of you sign these for the pieces."

First Billy, then Mule, bend over the desk and sign their names. They bring the guard belts around their middles, adjust the hooks for size, and straighten out their coats.

"Here's a clip each. Put it in your pocket."

They do so. The chief reaches in another drawer and pulls out two SP arm bands. He ties them on their arms.

"So there you are," says the chief, standing back and looking at them. "One minute you're sleeping it off in the TV room or shootin' craps in the reefer and the next minute you're the sheriff of Cochise."

The yeoman yawns audibly.

"Now do you have any questions?" asks the chief. "Everything clear?"

Billy and Mule nod.

"Let me tell you something else off the record. The old man and his old lady have a personal interest in this case. You know. So you fuck up and you know what."

"Yeah," says Mule. "We can give our hearts to Jesus."

"'Cause your asses will belong to the old man," finishes the chief.

The chief turns to Meadows and shouts, "Okay shitbird, on your feet!"

Meadows snaps out of the chair and comes to an awkward shaky attention.

"These two guys are taking you to Portsmouth. This is Petty Officer Buddusky and this is Petty Officer Mulhall."

"Yes, sir," says Meadows in a weak voice.

"Do you know why they're the chasers?"

"What are chasers, sir?"

"Guys that take you to the brig. Know why these guys are taking you?"

"No, sir."

"'Cause they're mean bastards when they want to be and they always want to be, and I give you my word they're not going to take any crap from a pussy like you. If they do, *they'll* get reamed and they know it. So if you have any smart-ass ideas you better forget them now. Keep your mouth shut and do what they tell you. Clear?"

"Yes, sir."

"What?"

"Yes sir!"

"Okay," the chief says. Then, to Billy and Mule "He's all yours."

They stand on either side of the prisoner. Together they walk out of the office and out of the building.

The MAA, his yeoman, and his messenger all go to the window and watch the trio march down the sidewalk to the carryall. Snow flurries have begun to blow. The chief shakes his head. "Billy Bad-Ass, the Black Mule, and the Charity Kid. What a tripod."

The yeoman says, "I wish I was going to Portsmouth instead of being stuck in this pig's ass of a place."

The messenger says nothing.

Three

The driver of the carryall puts his white hat on the back of his head to show that he's not afraid of any chickenshit Shore Patrol. He lights a cigarette without offering any around and double-clutches with a vengeance. The marine guard at the gate waves them by and the driver slows down to check the action on the strip, a block of sleazy bars, clothing stores, and locker clubs with signs: CIVVIES FOR RENT. The strip hangs from the gate of the naval base like a cigarette from a lower lip. When the carryall approaches the end of the strip, the driver rams it into high gear and continues to the downtown Greyhound terminal.

At the terminal they disembark and Mule says to the driver, "Sorry, son, I don't have any change." The driver slams the door shut and lays a bit of the taxpayers' rubber on the street when he leaves. They walk into the terminal to get out of the cold, and are noticed immediately by the people waiting for their buses and by other sailors especially who turn their heads against the backs of their seats, pretending to be asleep. Billy leaves Meadows with Mule and gets coffee to go in Styrofoam cups rather than sit in the coffee shop and perhaps spoil someone's lunch. They lean against the twenty-five-cent luggage lockers and sip their hot coffee.

When their bus is announced, Billy asks Meadows, "Do you need to go to the head?"

"No, sir," says Meadows.

"Be sure because from now on whenever you go to the head one of us will be with you."

"I'm not going to kill myself," says Meadows.

"I don't think so either," says Billy, "but you know how it is."

"Yeah well, I don't need to use the head anyway."

They board the bus and take the straight-across seat in the rear, Meadows sitting between Mule and Billy. Billy removes the cuffs from Meadows' wrists so that if there is an accident he will have the use of both hands. The three feel strange to each other. They don't know what to talk about, they are not sure how to behave. They are conspicuous and they wish the other passengers would mind their own business and let them carry out this detail. So for an hour and a half they do nothing but sit still and be transported from Norfolk to Richmond, a stretch of terrain that does little to lift the human heart.

In Richmond the train station is a relic, a cathedral to a religion proven false. A baroque ceiling over seventy-five feet high looms above the three of them like a gigantic bird of death as they walk across the long waiting room to the boarding gate. High frosted windows and grimy Venetian blinds block out the light of day. The station is not crowded, but what people are there, sitting in the massive blocks of wood-and-red padding arranged back-to-back in sixes and twos, lift their heads from their newspapers or stop their conversation in order to observe and conjecture about this free and unexpected drama of crime and punishment that has fallen their way. A little Negro girl pokes her mother's arm and points at them.

The men walk across the floor in step. They stand self-consciously among the crowd waiting for doors E and F to open. Billy sidles up to a marble stanchion and stands with his gun against it, out of view. Mule moves from side to side on the balls of his feet. Meadows holds the handcuffs close to his middle and as always directs his eyes to the floor. A long line of children, forty of them perhaps, two abreast, about five or six years old, are on a tour of the station. Around their necks are hung white cardboards with their names printed in black Marks-A-Lot: Rachael, Roberti, Bill, Marco, Desiree, Dick. They are led by their teacher, a tired woman in her mid-twenties who wears sunglasses on her forehead. She has three little helpers who are only a few years older than the rest of the children but they manage to keep the others in line. They fall silent as they pass the prisoner and his guards and they stare at them. The adults, who have been watching out of the corners of their eyes, shush the children when they stare and point.

Finally, the doors swing open and the crowd shifts its attention to getting aboard and seated. They walk down a long gloomy tunnel divided into two lanes by metal posts and a running chain. Two parallel rows of lights in the ceiling glow feebly. A conductor directs them to turn left at the door marked "Track 5." They go up a steep ramp and see daylight at the end of it. A frail old couple are struggling to push their luggage cart up the ramp. The man is thin and wears an oversized brown gabardine suit. The woman must be grandmother to a number of people.

Mule says to them, "Could you use a little help with that thing?"

"Well, it *is* heavy," says the grandmother.

Mule takes the cart and pushes it to the top of the ramp for them. They thank him and later he says to Billy, "There you are, another good deed performed by our fighting men of the US Navy."

They board the train and sit down in an end seat where Meadows has a seat to himself and Billy and Mile can sit facing him. Meadows looks at them, from one to the other and back again, as though waiting for some order. The other passengers find seats away from the three. They do not want to interfere unwittingly with the workings of military justice. Besides, they are curiously afraid of the trio.

The train jerks and then pulls away slowly. Billy and Mule remove their guard belts, take off their peacoats, and readjust the belts to their waists. They put the ammo clips in their jumper pockets and put their coats on the rack above them. Meadows looks uncomfortable in his peacoat.

"You wanna take yours off?" asks Billy.

"Yes, sir," says Meadows.

Billy undoes the cuffs, takes the coat, and puts it in the rack. He does not replace the handcuffs. Instead he stuffs them into the duffel bag beneath his seat. "Don't try any funny stuff," he says to Meadows.

"No, sir."

Billy takes a paperback copy of *The Centaur* out of his bag and begins to read.

Meadows looks out the window, his face against the heel of his palm. Mule watches Meadows. The industrial eyesores of any city pass by outside the window: Royal Pipe Supply, East Coast Restaurant Appliances, Frontier Aluminum, Inc., cranes in a junkyard. A flock of birds flies over a frozen pond and rises and falls as rhythmically as a conductor's baton.

Billy reads forty pages and closes his book, placing it on the seat next to him. Meadows is still looking out of the window with a trancelike intensity. Mule has been dozing but now wakes up. Billy holds his cigarette pack out to Meadows.

"Weed?"

"Thank you."

He gives one to Mule and lights all three on the same match. They sit and smoke.

"Well, Mule, heading north, huh?"

"Yeahhh, man."

"Some of my old stompin' grounds," says Billy. "Where are you from, Meadows?"

"Huh?"

"Where are you from?"

"Camden, New Jersey, sir."

"Hell, you don't have to 'sir' us. We're enlisted men, same as you. Call me Billy and call him Mule."

"Really?" says Meadows. He is surprised. Suddenly he wants to talk. "Where are you from, Billy?" he asks.

"Born and raised in the coal fields of Andoshen, P.A., only a few hours from Camden."

"Not much ocean 'round there, huh?"

"Not much of anything, even coal."

"Have you ever been to New England?"

"Sure."

"New Hampshire?"

"Yep."

"Is it nice?"

"Very nice, both summer and winter. Quiet little burgs, winding roads and trees that change colors when the seasons change. Very nice up there."

"Have you ever been to . . . Portsmouth?"

"Yes. Yes, I have."

Meadows tries to smile, but it comes out lopsided.

"I guess I won't get much chance to see the scenery."

"Where are you from, Mule?" asks Billy.

"Bogalusa, above N'Orleans."

"Hot down there, ain't it?"

"Yeah. Look, Meadows, I just gotta ask you. Why you figure they put the cock to you?"

Meadows puts his hand to his mouth. "I don't know. Maybe because of the polio thing. In the brig a guy told me it was because of the old man's wife and because he's a real law-and-order nut and thinks the kids today are getting away with murder, rioting 'n all. Hell, I was never even near a riot in my life. I don't have any opinions on anything yet."

"Did you have a record before this?" asks Billy.

"Not with the navy. Got into trouble a couple of times with the cops before I enlisted."

"What for?"

"Shoplifting. Small stuff. Never was in jail or anything."

"Well, they sure put the cock to you."

"Not much I can do about it. I don't think the law officer they assigned me wanted to do as much as maybe he could have. You know? I thought he was afraid of the old man. Didn't want to contradict him."

"You could have had a civilian lawyer if you'd wanted one," says Billy.

"Oh, yeah? I didn't know that."

"Well, you coulda."

"They cost money though, and, well, everything's so damn involved. Besides, who'da thought they'd do this?"

Billy shifts in his seat. "Why'd you do it kid? Were you that hard up for coin?"

"That's just it. I didn't need the money. I hardly ever even went out on liberty except maybe to a movie. Anyone can tell you that."

"Then how come?" asks Mule.

"They got a name for it. Kleptomaniac. I know I'm one of them. It was the same way with shoplifting before. I used to steal junk I didn't need. Quart bottles of hair tonic, model cars, books, crap like that. I was sorry for stealing the money, but I swear to you—I didn't even want it. I had money on the books even, from not collecting my full pay. 'Course, that's gone now because I got forfeiture of all pay and everything."

"Jesus," says Mule. "Eight years for forty bucks you didn't ever get. They sure put the cock to you, lad."

"Yeah," says Meadows.

They stop talking. Billy resumes his reading. Soon Meadows is asleep his head against the cold windowpane. The monotonous frozen countryside rolls by outside. Mule nudges Billy with his elbow and whispers, "Hey Billy."

"What?"

"You're a smart guy. This kleptomaniac business, what's it all about?"

"It's a sickness in the head. Means you can't help yourself from stealing stuff."

"What d'you mean, can't help yourself?"

"You don't want to do it but you got to do it anyway to get it out of your system. Like jerking off. It's a job for a psychiatrist."

"You figure an enlisted man can have it, same as an officer?"

Billy laughs. "Hell yes, we all put our pants on one leg at a time, didn't anyone ever tell you that?"

"You know, a couple of years ago, and this was in Norfolk too, a lieutenant supply officer lifted six thou and went over the hill. They nailed him two months later shacked up in Seattle with a red-headed whore. You know what happened?"

"No."

"They court-martialed him and told him to resign his commission and pay back the dough—you know, dollar down, dollar a week. Because they said his mind was all messed over. I heard he's running a beer bar in Portland now with the same red-headed whore."

"Makes you want to shit in your flat hat, doesn't it?"

"This Meadows kid's mind is as messed over as that lieutenant's. How come they didn't ask him to resign his rank of seaman?"

"You asking me?"

"No," says Mule.

It is fifteen minutes before they speak again.

"It beats the hell out of sitting in Shit City, though, don't it?" says Billy.

"Yeah, I guess so."

"There's a lot to be said for a detail like this," says Billy, looking out of the window. "No port and starboard watches, open gangplank, decent chow. As a way of life, it beats suicide."

"At least we get a long train ride. Man, I love trains."

"Who don't?"

"Yeah, I was always hangin' around the tracks when I was a kid," says Mule. "When we heard the train, we'd run up to the tracks and sometimes there would be bums riding in these big open cars full of sugar beets. They'd throw beets at us kids. We thought they were heroes, real big shots, and I guess it made them feel good to be looked up to for the first time in their lives and be able to give things away to kids. They'd throw a mess of beets over the side. Tasted like hell, but it was something for nothing. We sure did love those bums and those trains. One of those bums coulda been my old man, all I know. He jumped a train one day and was gone. I don't blame him. Man's gotta breathe his own air. But the bastard left us in a bad way. I'm an AFDC kid. You know what that is?"

"Huh?"

"I didn't think so. An Aid-to-Families-of-Dependent-Children kid. That means my mother was getting AFDC money from the parish, which most of the times was better than the old man would have gave us. But it ain't no fun to have to walk miles in stinking heat with your momma and three other kids to a smelly old parish welfare building and sit in a stuffy room in rickety seats with all the other poor mouths and wait for some white chick to come down and call out your name over a microphone and make you feel like you got a hell of a nerve living. Mulhall. God, when they called out that name for all to hear and my momma and us kids had to stand up and walk to a little booth where this wilted white chick would try to look sympathetic. I just wanted to crawl up my own ass and disappear. I think ever since I was ten I've been on the shy side of puking up my guts. Mulhall. Some rich old Irishman, I guess, from a hundred and fifty years ago. Mulhall AFDC. I think I better shut the hell up, man."

"Well, there's nothing like a train, though," says Billy, and lights another cigarette. "There was a freight yard a block away from our place in Andoshen, next to the icehouse. That's where I picked up my sex education. Those cars were our playpens. We'd climb into a boxcar that wasn't locked and sit with our legs dangling over the side and dream we were off traveling somewhere. Inside there was always excelsior and black packaging wire and cardboard. And those boxcars always smelt nice. I coulda *lived* in a boxcar. Christ, they were great for cowboys and Indians and cops and robbers and all that stuff climbing up and down the ladders and running across the top or crawling under the bottom." Billy laughs out loud, and Meadows stirs, but continues to sleep. He lowers his voice. "I remember once a friend was looking for me and I was right above him on top of the car. I pissed on his head. Just being crazy. Gene Franco. Wound up in reform school. A lot of my pals wound up in reform schools. I was lucky I guess."

"You ever get back to the old place?"

"No. To tell you the truth, Mule, better things were expected of me back there than to be a lifer in the navy. Everybody wanted me to be a teacher."

"Hell, my momma can't brag enough about me. She tells everybody all the places I go and how many men are under me and like that. The hometown boy has made the Great Equality Scene. Shee-it."

"Well, my folks wanted me to get an education. They worked hard for it and I just said fuck a whole bunch of education. So my kid brother got the education. Turned him into a jerk, last time I talked to him."

"Ever sorry you didn't take it?"

"Hell, no. If I did I'd be sitting behind a desk with a belly falling over my belt. The hell with that. I'll let you in on a secret: I love the goddamn navy. I get three squares, a pad to lie down on, roof over my head, tuxedo to wear. We're living high off the hog. I wouldn't know what to do if I wasn't in the navy. Go from door to door and ask if anyone had any signaling to do, I guess."

"There sure are the benies if you don't have an education. Hell, I bet between the two of us there ain't many places we ain't been."

"Or booze we ain't drunk."

"Or broads we ain't laid."

"Yeah, there's much to be said for the navy," says Billy.

"Except for the occupational hazards."

"Well, but you get that on the outside too."

"Not like here."

"You mean this detail?"

"Yeah."

"This ain't one of the happiest details I ever drew," says Billy.

"Me neither. But at least it's lucky for him it's us and not a couple marines. How come they didn't use grunts? Don't they usually?"

"I don't know. I guess they figured Meadows was small potatoes."

"He don't strike me as the violent type. A Wave could handle him."

"That's why they picked us," says Billy, and Mule laughs.

"It's lucky for him they didn't use grunts. Those bastards are sadistic."

"Yeah, they train 'em that way. Train 'em to enjoy other people's pain. That's *their* occupational hazard."

"I'd be in mind to get one of 'em later and put a hurt on 'em if I was ever in the brig and they beat up on me."

"I remember when I was on the *Intrepid* they had a mean brig there. These Pfc.'s would march the brig guys back and forth across the hangar deck. Some punk Pfc. would stand on the deck at the top of a ladder and there'd be a line of prisoners at the foot of the ladder on the deck below. One by one the guys would yell, 'Sir, may I come up the ladder, *sir?*' The grunt would say, 'Come maggot,' and the guy would race up the ladder, clattering like hell, and put his nose against the bulkhead. Each guy had a swab and had his white hat pulled down over his ears. The grunt would shout, 'Well?' Then the guy would say '*Sir,* may I proceed *sir?*' The grunt would say 'Go, maggot.' Finally, they would march across the hangar deck shouting every five seconds 'Gangway—*prisoner!*' Gangway—*prisoner!* Gangway—*prisoner!*' Jesus, I hate to see sailors having to take that from those marine bastards. Used to send a chill down my spine."

"It's the power, man. Those grunts come into the Corps outa the poolroom where even the rack boy don't pay no attention to 'em. All of a sudden they got power over the poor brig bastards and they grind 'em under their heel."

"That's why they go ape in Vietnam. If they sit around too long without killing something, they go out and find something to kill. Don't matter an ox, a woman, a baby. Over there a grunt can kill a whole family of civilians and get six months in the can, and everybody will sigh and say, 'Thank God this isn't happening in the United States.' They figure what's another gook more or less."

"You got it there," says Mule. "I mean, after all, those gooks don't even *look* like us, man."

"And a kid like this they give eight years to for nothing. Ain't that a bitch?"

"Billy, what do you think about us doing something for the kid?"

"Like what?"

"I dunno. He said Camden's his hometown. What about we stop over and let him see his folks?"

Billy thinks for a moment and says, "What the hell, we got time to burn. Let's take him home and give him a few hours. We can always catch the next train."

Billy reaches over and shakes Meadows.

"Hey, Meadows, you got any family in Camden?"

Meadow says groggily, "What?"

"You got kin in Camden?"

"Yeah, my mother."

"You wanna stop for a few hours and see her?"

"You mean it?"

"Sure, as long as you behave yourself."

"Ain't it against the regulations?"

"Well, hellfire, how do we know?" says Billy.

"I don't want you guys getting in trouble."

"Don't sweat it," says Mule.

"Well, if you think it's all right . . ."

"Just you behave yourself."

"I will. Jeez, you guys are all right. My mom will sure be glad to see me."

"Does she know what's happening?"

"I wrote and told her about the trouble I was in but I haven't written since then. So she still thinks I'm being court-martialed in Norfolk."

"Man, you shoulda written," says Billy.

"I can tell her when I see her."

"That's what I mean," says Billy.

Billy and Mule give only passing notice to the landmarks that slowly pass outside the windows. They have seen them hundreds of times before, always like this, through the windows of a train, a bus, a plane. If pressed, they can identify them, and do so for Meadows, who is now in Washington D.C., for the second time in his life, having gone through once before on a late-night bus bound for Norfolk. Neither Billy nor Mule has ever been to the Washington Monument, the Lincoln Memorial, the White House, or any of the other sights. Meadows finds that impossible to believe.

"But I bet I've been in every bar within six blocks of every station and terminal in town, and that's *something,* I guess," says Billy.

"And I bet I know where I can get laid in this town," adds Mule.

"Yeah, but to be here in the capital of the greatest nation on earth and not *see* anything . . ." says Meadows.

"What's to see? Great blocks of stone? Shitfire," says Mule. The train grinds to a stop. It is almost 6:30 p.m. Billy consults his timetable and says, "We have about enough time for some chow.

Then we can catch a train to Philly and grab a bus to Camden. Whaddaya want to eat, Larry?"

"Gee, I don't know."

"Well, you can call this shot. Anything you want."

"I could go for a couple of cheeseburgers and fries and a big chocolate shake."

"Look," says Billy "is your word worth anything?"

"What do you mean?"

"Just what I said."

"What an awful thing to say! Sure it is, as good as the next guy's."

"As good as the next guy? That ain't worth much. The next guy's a prick."

"All right then, *better* than the next guy's if it comes to that. I wouldn't go back on my word if that's what you mean, and I don't remember ever doing it either. 'Course I don't remember being asked *not* to."

"I want you to give us your word you won't try to escape in Washington. If you do that, we can stow these damn cannons and armbands in a locker. Because it's no fun having to eat with artillery on your hip and all."

"Hell," says Larry, "I wouldn't try to escape. That would be like admitting I was guilty."

"Did anyone ever tell you you watch too much TV?" says Billy.

They take his word and put their guns, armbands, and AWOL bags in a fifty-cent locker at the terminal. They feel pounds lighter and walk jauntily now, like sailors. They pass by two restaurants that look as though they wouldn't have good cheeseburgers and approach a third that has possibilities. They stop in front and study it.

"What do you think?" Billy asks Meadows.

"I don't know. Looks okay."

"Just so the bastards give the cheese a chance to melt on the burger is all," says Mule.

"They better toast the buns and have grilled onions," says Billy. "And I like my fries nice and gold and greasy."

"I'm more worried about the shakes. What if they're not thick?"

"Son-of-a-bitch," says Billy, "we're either gonna have to make the plunge or go hungry."

They go inside and order and wait for the food, savoring the odors of the place. Everything is to their liking. This is an excellent cheeseburger place.

"You know," says Larry, "you can't fall into any old place and expect it to be good. You gotta check it out real careful."

Billy holds his milk shake up as if it were a fine wine. "I must have had one of these once, but damned if I can remember when. They're *good,* you know. Put milk in 'em, do they?"

Larry laughs at him.

Out in the street again, they raise their collars around their necks and put on their gloves.

"We still have time for a beer," says Billy, looking at his watch.

"I ain't old enough," says Larry.

"For what?"

"For a beer."

"Hellfire, *everyone's* old enough for a beer."

They go into a bar, Billy saying, "I know this place. This is a good place to have a beer, nice and quiet."

They are the only customers. They go to the bar, sit on stools, and Billy says, "Hi there, Ed, I'll have thirty cents' worth of beer in a glass, the same for my shipmates here."

"Ed don't work here no more and lemme see your I.D.'s," says the barman.

"How come?" says Billy.

"'Cause this kid ain't twenty-one," says the barman, tilting his head toward Larry.

"Look, pal," says Billy, "this man just got back from nine months off the coast of Vietnam, lobbing shells over there to blow the ass offa the VC. so your bar here can be safe for democracy. Just like us. So why can't he have a friggin' beer at least, just like us?"

"Look yourself, *pal*," says the barman. "The law says I *hafta* serve him," nodding toward Mule, "and it says I *can't* serve him," nodding toward Meadows. "You figure it out."

Mule says, "Mr. Citizen Bartender, tell you what to do. Take your beers and ram 'em up your ass sideways and maybe then you'll be able to fart 'America, the Beautiful,' motherfucker."

The barman's hand drops below the bar.

"Whoa there, Sunshine," says Billy. "We're on our way, peace and quiet, law and order. You can take your hand off the horsecock you're holding under the bar. You know the three of us would be able to cream you anyway."

"How do you know I don't have something that barks here and bites over there?" asks the barman.

Mule backs away from the bar. Meadows is dumbfounded.

"Ho, ho, ho, this redneck's talking about *firearms,*" says Billy. "But I happen to know there ain't nothing under that bar but wood, cause I happened to be in here one night when a certain sailor had it laid upalongside the head. Whaddaya think of that, redneck?"

The barman puts his hands back on the bar and says, "Let's be friends, sailor. The boss'd lose his license if I serve the kid."

"I should *give* you a puck in the snoot," says Billy.

"I'd call the Shore Patrol," says the barman.

"Listen to *that!'* says Billy. "We *are* the Shore Patrol. I'm beginning to think I should cut out your rotten belly."

"Look, let's be friends," says the barman, truly worried now. "I'm just a family man trying to make a living for his kids."

"I was wondering when we'd get that," says Mule.

"C'mon, guys," says Meadows, plucking them both by the sleeves. "I don't want an old beer anyway. Don't start a fuss. It ain't worth it, really it ain't."

He tugs and coaxes them out the door. Mule lets fly a parting remark: "When your wife told me what a mean bastard you were she got so mad she damn near bit off my peter."

Outside they hurry away from the bar just in case he does put in a call to the Shore Patrol. Mule and Larry are coming to understand why their new friend is called Bad-Ass. Larry says, "Gee Billy, cool down, I'm glad you did stow your gun. You woulda blown off his head."

Billy snaps his fingers and says, "Damn, wouldn't you know it? When you could use a gun you never have one."

"I didn't want a crummy old beer anyway."

"Well, you're gonna *have* one."

"Aw, c'mon, Billy, please, no fuss."

"I think the kid has a good point there," says Mule.

Billy speaks with resolve. "This kid ain't leaving D.C. until he has a belly full of beer."

They come to a corner store and Billy leaves them to go inside. He comes out with three six-packs of the "local beer," and together they find an alley and sit on wooden crates at the rear entrance to some small shop. They lean their backs against a dumpster and open up three cans. "Here's to you, kid, drink hardy," says Billy.

They sit in freezing weather and drink beer. They finish one round, throw the empties into the dumpster and open another.

"I'm not sure I can finish this," says Larry. "It's too damn cold."

"Beer is *supposed* to be cold," says Billy.

"No. It's too cold *outside!*"

"Then you don't have to worry about the beer getting warm."

Billy takes a long swallow and sighs appreciatively. "Nothing like it," he says. "I'd advise against hard liquor, but there's nothing like beer. 'Course the hop will never surpass the grape, but it's still pretty damn good."

"But I'm beginning to wonder if we *have* to sit out here and freeze our balls off in order to drink it," says Mule. "This is pretty ridiculous, you know. Sitting here against a garbage can and it's colder than a witch's tit out. Maybe we can smuggle it on the train."

Billy looks at his watch. "Our train just left."

"Well, that's outstanding, that's real outstanding," says Mule. "And we were supposed to take the kid home."

"I'm sorry, Larry, but look, I have an idea. We got time up the gump stump, we're on per diem, let's just check the hell into a hotel and catch the early train tomorrow morning. That's Sunday. Would that be okay?"

"Sure," says Meadows. "If it's all right with you, I don't mind. Is it in the regulations?"

"You know, kid," says Mule, "you coulda been an admiral. Shoulda been anyway. Let's get into a warm room with sheets on the bed, for Chrissake."

They pick up their AWOL bags at the terminal and check into the Lennox Hotel, a third-rater, but a healthy cut above the navy Y, to which they are accustomed.

In the small room there are two beds, a double and a cot, which doesn't look comfortable. Billy throws his AWOL bag on the cot and says, "I'll take this. You two take the double."

Mule removes Billy's bag and puts his own on the cot. "I'll take it. You two can sleep in the bed."

Now Meadows sits on the cot and tries to bounce up and down on it. It has no spring in it. "I think I should take the cot," he says, "'Cause I'm the youngest."

"No, *I'm* taking the cot," says Mule, "because I'm the *blackest.* You two sleep together."

"Goddamn it," says Billy, "if I hear one more racial remark a certain black bastard is gonna get a karate chop right across the apple. I'm the goddamn honcho here and I'm taking the cot."

"Well, fuck you a whole bunch of cots," says Mule. "I'm a first class too and I'll be *damned* if you're gonna tell me where to sleep."

"I think since I'm the youngest I should have the cot," says Meadows carefully.

"Who in the hell asked you what in the hell you think?" says Billy.

"I'm sorry," says Meadows. "I didn't mean any offense."

"Look, can we forget about the damn cot till later and just sit anywhere and have a damn beer? This is the stupidest conversation I've ever been in."

They take off their peacoats, pull off their jumpers, and sit around drinking beer and smoking cigarettes in their T-shirts.

"Ah, is this the life or what?" says Billy, putting his stocking feet under the radiator that hisses beneath the fogged-up window.

"Sure beats freezing your ass off in some goddamn alley," agrees Mule.

"And it sure beats being back at Shit City."

"It sure beats being at Portsmouth too," says Meadows, who is not used to beer and feels a little light-headed. His statement spoils the illusion of liberty and leisure. Billy flips his empty into a wastebasket and pulls the tabs, with angry yanks, off three more cans. He passes them around and says, "Let's make a deal. Let's nobody mention Portsmouth again for the whole trip. Or else I punch him in the mush. That's the deal."

"You sure are a hard son-of-a-bitch, ain't you?" says Mule.

"It's your goddamn fault."

"I gotch your goddamn *fault*—dangling."

"Well then, hand it over here and I'll slam the goddamn window down on it!"

Mule and Billy look at each for a moment and when they see there is nothing more to say, they break up in laughter. The expression on Larry's face shows that he is having a difficult time understanding them.

When it is quiet in the room, Larry says, "Do you guys mind if I ask something?"

"As long as you don't mention you-know-what."

"That thing at the bar, what was that all about?"

"What do you mean?"

"That whole thing. He was only doing his job. I don't blame him for not giving me a beer."

"Yeah, but look at the way he treated Mule. He said in so many words that the only reason he would serve him is because he *had* to."

"But look at what *you* said, Mule. About his wife. That was awful and it wasn't even true."

"It'd be more awful if it was true," says Mule.

"It was funny as hell, anyway," says Billy and he and Mule crack up again.

"Still, though," says Larry earnestly, "he was wrong in what he said, but so were you. Don't you see, when you threatened him and bad-mouthed him and everything, you were no better than he was. Worse, even, because at least he was looking out for his job and good jobs are hard to find."

"What a bunch of bullshit!" says Billy. "I'm sick to death of everybody just 'doing their job.' It's like, 'I can use and abuse you and beat on you twice on weekends, but I'm only Doing My Job, man.' They're doing their jobs, all right. Like Napoleon. Some of these days people are gonna hafta forget their jobs and start thinking about their lives. Nobody knows how long he's gonna live. What a kick in the ass to spend a whole lifetime being a schmuck just 'cause you're doing your stinking job. Then you die and somebody else does your job and your life didn't count for a fart."

Mule says, "For once I agree with Bad-Ass. Every damn racist, crook and bastard who's a drag on the world is just doing his job, which is something the rest of the country is supposed to admire him for because what kind of a prick wouldn't do his *job?*"

"But look at you guys, for instance," says Larry. "You're only doing *your* jobs."

The air is dead for a long moment before Billy says, "God-damn, Larry, you got a helluva knack for bringing things to a close, if you know what I mean."

"What do you mean?"

"Nothing," says Mule. "Don't worry about it."

Mule pulls his jumper over his head, adjusts his neckerchief and pulls on his peacoat. "I'm goin' for more beer," he says.

Billy is slumped in the stuffed easy chair. He puts his beer can on the arm and signals with his hands, holding them close in front of him: BRAVO, YANKEE, BRAVO, YANKEE.

Mule says, "Yeah, I'll see you in a few minutes."

After he is gone, Larry says, "Ain't this something, sitting in Washington D.C., drinking beer and smoking cigarettes? You don't know how great this is for me."

"Were they rough on you in Norfolk?" Billy asks.

"You know, they really were, when I was waiting for the court-martial and all. And I couldn't figure out why. I never did anything to any of them and I always tried to do what they told me, but still there was always somebody giving me a poke in the ribs or a kick in the ass. You know what one of them said?"

"What?"

"He asked me if I believed in Jesus Christ and I said yes and he said that from now on *he* was Jesus Christ and that I shouldn't forget it. Can you imagine that? That's awful. Boy. He better hope the chaplain don't catch him at that."

Billy laughs and says, "How many navy chaplains do you know up close, Larry?"

"None, I guess, except for going to services on Sunday."

"Well, I've known a bunch of them and they were all Texas Baptists who like to stand on the bridge with the old man and wear aviator sunglasses and wish to hell they were line officers so they could boss somebody around. I've seen them fink on enlisted men lots of times. If you told a chaplain what the grunts did to you, he'd probably say it was good training for a young seaman. You got to learn, Larry, that people ain't what they appear to be."

"Maybe not, but I don't believe that about the chaplains. I think they probably screen 'em very carefully before they take 'em into the navy. And it takes a lot of spunk and devotion to be a chaplain."

"It takes what? Christ, they never had it so good. Their own stateroom, sharp clothes, people kissing their asses. Any cheap Bible thumper on the outside has all the qualifications of a navy chaplain. The *real* navy, Larry, is man's work. Men and a ship and the sea. Anything extra, like chaplain shit, just clutters up something good and simple."

"Don't you think you could count on one, if you had, you know, personal problems?"

"There's only one person you can count on—yourself. And if you come to the point where you can't count on yourself, then you might as well fold up your pennants."

"Your signal pennants, you mean? I'd sure like to know how to do that. How long did it take you to learn?"

"Not long. Depends on how much you like doing it. I go for it. It's like being able to talk a second language, but better. It's great for talking to yourself."

"How can you signal yourself?"

"Well, you . . . 1 don't know, you just do it. And it's great when you want to say something, but don't want to. Like maybe if you pissed me off, I might want you to shut up, but I wouldn't want to say it so I'd semaphore it."

"Wouldn't do much good if I didn't understand it."

"That don't matter. The sending is what's important."

"If this didn't happen, I probably woulda struck for signalman."

"Well, hell, it's not hard. Let me teach you the hand signals and by the end of the trip, you'll have it down cold."

Billy and Larry stand side by side in the middle of the room.

"Okay," says Billy, "now if you pretend you're a clock and your hands are the hands of a clock, A is like twenty to six. B is quarter to six, C is ten to, and D is six o'clock. Okay, now you try it."

Slowly and judging the positions very carefully, Larry goes from A through D.

"That was damn good," says Billy. "You probably have a flair for this kind of thing. Lotsa guys are like that. I am. All right, now for E you start working down the other side. E is ten after six, F, a quarter after, G twenty after. The rest of them are difficult to learn so we'll get to those later. Let's run through what we've got."

Facing each other and holding their arms straight out, Billy and Larry run from A through G. During the practice Mule comes in with three six-packs and says, "What the hell is this? Russian navy Bol Shoy Ballet?"

"Yeah, and ain't your name Phyllis? So fill us a beer, cunt," says Billy.

They lie around and drink beer. Meadows cannot remember ever drinking ten cans of beer before, all by himself. He is definitely drunk, he decides. The other two show signs of becoming that way. Larry, with some effort to organize his mouth, speaks: "I don't like to hammer away at one subject, *but. . .*"

"There's always a *but,*" says Mule. "'I believe in equal rights,' says the Senator, *'but!'*"

"There you go again. I wish you'd forget about your goddamn complexion for ten minutes running."

"I was talkin' about one of the major issues of the day, shitferbrains."

"I gotch your major issue of the day—swinging."

"Well, hand it over here and I'll slap it on this goddamn radiator and fry it."

"Gentlemen, gentlemen, please, I beg of you," says Meadows, standing up and swinging his arms, trying to parody a parliamentarian.

"Get a load of this," says Mule.

"I was about to say," says Larry, still playing his role, "before I was so *rudely* interrupted, thank you very much, that here we are on the *pulse* of the world. A lot of poor kids in Europe would give their eye teeth to be here, and here we sit in a hotel room. It ain't right."

"We could go back to the alley," says Billy.

"The hell with that," says Mule.

"You know, guys," says Larry, growing serious now, "there's no telling when or *if* I'll ever be in Washington again. I think I'd like to see a statue or something."

"You're damn right you would and you *will,*" says Billy, getting to his feet. "There's a brochure here on the desk that lists the sights. We're gonna go see us a few of them *right now.* Jumpers on! We're gonna show Meadows the goddamn Pentagon."

And the Pentagon is the first sight they visit. They walk around it slowly, in awe of the invisible power that emanates from within. "Gee," says Meadows, "that's where it all happens. That's where they say, 'Land the marines at Lebanon,' and sure enough the marines go land in Lebanon."

"I'd hate to bust your bubble on that one, but when they landed the marines at Lebanon they had to dodge the swimmers and when they got on the beach there was a gook there to sell 'em a cold Coke."

They went to the Supreme Court Building and stood at the bottom of the long impressive flight of steps. "Some important people have walked up these steps," says Meadows.

"Boy, I wonder what it takes to become a Supreme Court judge."

"An in with the President is all," says Mule. "He picks them."

"Hey, how come I didn't appeal *my* case to the Supreme Court. Boy, am I dumb!"

"Affirmative," says Billy. "The Supreme Court is only for civilians."

"That doesn't seem fair," says Larry.

"Well, the navy has different laws and everything from the outside," says Mule.

"In eight years I'll be a civilian again and *then* I'll appeal to the Supreme Court."

"You do that, Clarence Darrow, maybe they'll shorten your sentence," says Billy.

In turn they visit the Washington Monument, the Lincoln Memorial, and the Jefferson Memorial, all deserted at this time of night. Larry feels proud to stand in front of them and says, "I wish we had a camera with a flash attachment. This is just like the slides we had in civics class. It's good to be an American, you know? And have all of this in common with other Americans."

"I heard that George Washington had wooden teeth," says Billy.

"Wooden teeth?" says Mule.

"That's what I heard."

"Well, in those days they didn't have regular enamel false teeth like today," says Larry reasonably. "What did you expect the poor guy to do? Eat baby food?"

"They didn't have baby food either. All I'm saying is what I heard," says Billy. "I don't give a rat's ass if he had teeth made of coal."

"You shouldn't say anything against George Washington, him being the father of our country and all," says Larry.

"What did I say? That he had wooden teeth. Is that a crime?"

"I heard he had slaves too," says Mule.

"Now don't *you* start that up again! Let's forget about fucking George Washington."

"Watch your language when you talk about him," says Meadows. "I don't care how big you are."

"Jesus Christ, you two bastards are driving me over the side! I used to be a quiet, normal person, like yesterday, even."

They drop the subject and walk away. Billy sets a fast pace and leaves Mule and Larry trailing six feet behind him.

"You know what I'd like to see?" says Larry. "The Tomb of the Unknown Soldier."

"We'll have to pass that one up," says Billy. "It's in Arlington and that's too much of a hassle. Besides they probably wouldn't let us in this late." Billy slows down and allows them to come abreast of him.

"I bet they found a lot of unknown soldiers," says Larry.

"What about sailors?" asks Mule.

"Well, them too, I guess," says Larry. "There's unknown sailors same as there's unknown soldiers."

"I guess all of us could lie in that tomb," says Billy.

"It doesn't matter much where you lie once you're dead."

"Don't tell that to a colored person," says Mule. "You know, during the riots when we were burning down every business what's been gouging us, we never burned down the business what's been gouging us the most for years—undertakers. Colored folks are *afraid* of dead people, man."

"I ain't afraid of dying," says Billy. "It's just that I'll be gone for sooooo long."

They save the big one for last: the White House. They stand at the south portico and Larry says, "There he is in there, the Commander-in-Chief."

"The Big Honcho," say Mule. "If he tells you to shit, you ask, 'How much and what color, sir?'"

"I wonder if he's awake," says Larry. "He probably went to bed. It's later than hell."

"Maybe he's up late working on some big deal."

"Like more benies for us."

"Hell, let's go up and knock on the door and introduce ourselves," says Billy. "He'd be happy to see a few guys from his command."

"Negative, negative, negative," says Mule.

They walk back to the hotel. On the way, Billy starts singing softly, *"Whaddaya do with a drunken sailor? Whaddaya do with a drunken sailor? Whaddaya do with a drunken sailor—earl—lye in the morn—ing?* "

The others join in and as they do, they throw their arms over each other's shoulders, with Billy in the middle and wearily make their way down the cold deserted street.

Put him in the long boat, make him bail'er
Put him in the long boat, make him bail'er
Put him in the long boat, make him bail'er.
Earl—lye in the morn—orn—ing

They stop at a traffic light and sing the refrain.

Yo——ho——up, she rises
Yo——ho——up, she rises
Yo——ho——up, she rises,
Earl—lye in the morn—orn—ing.

As the light changes, a blue Chevy turns the corner in front of them and the driver shouts out of the window without slowing down, "Hey, baby, wanna blow job?" The car continues down the street.

"Now I wonder," says Billy, "which of us that young gentleman was addressing."

They sing no more. Instead they hurry out of the cold night and back to their hotel. They take off their uniforms and carefully fold them inside out. All three, tired at the end of this long day, stand in their skivvies in front of the beds.

"This being a tourist is damned hard work," says Billy. *"I'm* bone-tired and I don't feel like arguing. I'm gonna take the cot."

"I really think I should take it," says Meadows. "I'm the youngest."

"Here we go again," says Billy.

"I'm not gonna sleep in the same bed with a white boy. I get the cot."

"Son-of-a-bitch, give me that pillow," says Billy and grabs a pillow from the bed. He rips off the blanket, wraps himself up in it, and lies in the corner of the floor. He punches the pillow twice, jams his head on it and turns his back on the other two.

"Well, I be goddamn," says Mule. He takes the other pillow from the bed, tears the blanket from the cot, and settles down in another corner on the floor.

Meadows watches all of this with what is now becoming a familiar sense of confusion. He sits on the bed and bounces. It is nice and soft. The other two pay no attention. He yearns to stretch out on the soft bed, but instead he takes the pillow from the cot and the extra blanket from the bottom drawer of the dresser and stretches out on the floor at the foot of the bed. No one has bothered to turn out the light.

They lie like this for five minutes, trying to sleep on the hard floor. Then Billy raises his head and looks at the other two. Mule raises his head, and finally Larry raises his, and all three look at each other for a moment in silence.

"I'll tell you two bastards something," says Billy. "I've traveled over a million miles by every kind of ve-hicle with all kinds of funny guys but you two take the fucking cake. There you got two nice beds. Neither of you slept on a bed between sheets for months, and here you lie on the floor. Incredible. Incredible."

"I gotch your incredible," says Mule. "You're the bastard started all this."

"Yeah, I knew it had to be my fault. Excuse me for breathing."

They punch their pillows again and try to sleep. Another five minutes pass before Billy jumps up, throws his blanket to the floor and almost in tears yells, "This is ridiculous, for Chrissake! What the hell are we trying to prove? I'm going to sleep on the goddamn cot and I'll do some dental work on any bastard who tries to stop me!"

"If any mother tries to sleep on that cot, he's gonna get a nutcracker sweet from me, personally," says Mule, going into a crouch.

Larry leaps between them and says, "Wait a minute, I think I have the answer. Why don't all three of us sleep in the big bed. It's too small lengthwise, but we can sleep *across* it."

The other two are willing to do anything to resolve the impasse so they all lie down across the bed. From their knees down, they hang out over the side of the bed.

After a long moment Mule says, "Jesus, how can a man sleep like this?"

"Wait a minute," says Larry, "I got another idea. You two just lie here peaceful."

He takes the cot and slides it next to the bed, but it is too low. Their heels only are supported by the cot.

"Wait a minute, wait a minute, I'm full of ideas," mutters Larry. He pulls out two dresser drawers, overturns them, and slides one under each of the two legs of the cot that are next to the bed. The edges of the bed and the cot now meet and form an incline so that the sleepers' legs are supported, at a slight angle. It will work only if all three sleep on their backs, but this is as close as they'll come to a peaceful solution, so they accept it. Larry turns out the light and crawls between the other two. They are soon asleep.

Four

In the morning their backs and legs ache. One by one, they inch across the cot on their behinds and stretch their limbs to work on the stiffness. They do not speak to each other. Larry's mouth feels as though he has Virginia Beach inside of it. Mule and Billy both have throbbing headaches. Larry turns on the cold water tap and drinks three glasses of water, belching loudly after the third. "Excuse me," he mumbles. Mule stands in front of the mirror and, bleary-eyed, massages his scalp. He farts. "Excuse me," he says. Billy lights up a cigarette and inhales deeply. He is thrown into a fit of grinding, heaving, devastating coughing. When it has passed, he gasps, "Excuse me."

They get black coffee in large containers at the terminal and drink it as they wait. Mule and Billy have once again strapped on their guns and fastened their arm bands. Nothing is done or said about the handcuffs. They board their train and take seats facing each other.

"Well, Larry," says Billy, "going home to see your mother, huh?"

"Yep, if you say so."

"Wake me up when we get to Philly. Then we'll grab a bus for Camden."

All three recline their seats as far back as they will go, and in a few minutes they are asleep.

Larry's house in Camden is a house without promise. After Sunday dinner no one kicks off his shoes and sprawls on the floor with the Sunday *Bulletin* comics in this house. Even its smells are not its own; it smells of strangers. Meadows reveals no great pleasure in seeing it again, yet he would give everything to be able to spend the next eight years here. To stay inside the kitchen at the table with the oilcloth cover, the flaking paint outside, the dirt yard outside, the filthy gutter outside, everything outside.

He looks into the kitchen now as his mother hurries to the bedroom and shuts the door. She turns and secures her rump-slumped chenille robe around her ample middle. She herds them into the kitchen. Billy notices a ratty windbreaker on the couch. She seats them at the rickety kitchen table and backs her rear end against the sink.

"Well, if this ain't a surprise, I'll tell you. You mighta called, you know. I paid my bill last month, so I think I'm still in the book. You pop in here early in the morning with two torpedoes, what do I think? I'm ready to have a heart attack. I'm not even gonna give you a cup of coffee till I get the whole scoop and nothing but the scoop."

"Well, Mom, remember I wrote you about my trouble? Didn't you get the letter?"

"Sure, I was gonna write just this after'. I got the letter on my bureau with the writing paper. Was gonna write just this after'. Sticky fingers again, huh?"

Meadows looks at the floor.

She speaks to Billy and Mule. "Inherited it from his old man. You couldn't offer him a drink he wouldn't steal the glass from you. Thiefed himself outa one job after another, miserable bum. But he was a helluva card. Laugh, you couldn't help but laugh at him. I was nutty about him when we got married, I'll have to admit that, I guess, miserable bum. Stole twelve years of my best, that was his biggest heist."

She bends forward in a pleading posture. "This kid's okay, though. Ask anyone. There ain't a mean bone in his body. Always the teacher's pet. He just has this thing, you know, with sticky fingers. Lotsa people are that way. His father, miserable bum, he was that way. Inherited it from him."

"You don't have to explain to us," says Billy. "We can't do anything."

She turns now to her son. "So what's the verdict? They kick you out of the navy? These guys bring you home or what?"

"Mom, it's worse than that."

"Whaddaya mean, worse?"

"I've been sentenced to eight years. These men are taking me to prison in Portsmouth. That's in New Hampshire."

"Eight years! Jesus, Mary 'n Joseph, you said all you did was sticky finger something from a store!"

"Well, it was forty bucks and it was a polio contribution box, that's the something."

"Yeah, I seen them things. I didn't think they held that much. Are you sure it was forty? Maybe somebody hiked the count on you so they could nail you one. Are you sure it was forty?"

"It don't matter how much it was, Mom."

"Whaddaya mean, don't matter? For two bucks, maybe, they're gonna give you eight years?"

"You see, Mrs. Meadows," says Billy, "military law doesn't have set punishment for different kinds of robbery like civilian law. It's whatever a court-martial says. I think the exact phrase is ' . . . shall be punished as a court-martial directs.' Which means they coulda given Larry life or let him go. That's the way it is in the service. If a review board don't lessen the sentence, that's it."

"Well, that's a helluva way for it to be. Here's a good kid never hurt anybody. And what a beautiful baby he was, never cried, always smiling. Chrissake, why'd they want to give a kid like this eight years?"

"I don't know, Mom," says Larry.

She paces the kitchen gesturing with her hands. "You know, a person's got some rights in this country. This ain't Russia where they can bust into your house in the middle of the night and cart you off to prison. A person's got some *rights* in America."

"Not in the service, he ain't," says Mule.

She turns her fury on Mule. "What the hell do *you* know about it! Suddenly everybody's an expert on rights. What are you, a Black Panther or something, you should tell me about my rights?"

"Mom! That's not fair. These guys have been good to me. They don't have nothing to do with it. They just take me there. It's their duty. They didn't have to bring me home on the way. They're sticking their necks way out to do this."

She puts a hand on Mule's shoulder. "I'm sorry," she says to him. "A mother's rage. You shouldn't pay no attention."

"Okay," says Mule.

"But I'll tell you this right now, I'm gonna write my congressman a letter or two. I got his name around here. He sent me a form letter once asking my opinions. I'm gonna crack off a zinger this afternoon. This ain't the American way of justice. Don't you worry, Lar baby, your mama's gonna look into this matter."

"Do you think we could have the coffee now?" asks Larry.

"I got some eggs and bread and spuds. I'll fix you a good breakfast at least. Wisht I had some bacon or something."

"Eggs and spuds'll be fine. A mess of them. Right, guys?"

"Right," say Billy and Mule.

She sets about making breakfast "Jesus, the neighborhood's changed since you been gone. Old Mr. Keller croaked, but he was almost eighty years old, he shoulda croaked, but remember Danny Cree?"

"Yeah, he was two years ahead of me in school."

"Dead. Was in a horrible car accident with his girlfriend. She only got banged up a little, but he was killed instantly. I saved you a clipping. It's around here somewhere."

Larry shakes his head. "Jeez, that's terrible. He was a nice guy. He could hook-shot with either hand."

"Yeah, and the Kowalicks moved to Passaic. Betty Bronson married a guy from Red Bank. Your old flame Mary Ellen McAboy got married too. Ho, ho, ho, didn't know that, did you? That struck a tender nerve. He used to have the hots for her," she says to the other two. "No gumption, though. You're better off. I heard it was a shotgun wedding. See, it coulda been *you* getting in trouble, saddled with a pregnant bride."

She gives them each a cup of coffee and puts the pot on the table. Larry wraps his hands around the cup. "Yeah, ain't I lucky," he murmurs.

A man appears in the kitchen doorway He looks spent, but not happily spent. With his appearance is the distinct introduction of body odor, and he reminds one of back rooms—gas stations, fire houses, pool halls. Billy runs his hand across his mouth and looks at Mule, who scratches his knee and looks away.

"Gotta cuppa that fer me, Leona?"

Mrs. Meadows looks at him and is reminded of the problem she had forgotten.

"Who are you?" asks Larry.

"Well, navy, I ain't exactly the gas man. Ha, ha, ha, ha!"

"Who is this guy?" Larry asks his mother.

Mrs. Meadows dishes out the eggs and potatoes. She is next to the toaster, waiting for the toast to pop up.

"Oh yeah, you never met Mr. Smith, did you, Lar? He's from the neighborhood. This is my kid Larry."

"Hyuh, Larry, give me five."

Larry refuses the outstretched hand.

"Sensitive. Very sensitive kid, Leona," says Mr. Smith.

"These are his two buddies from the navy."

"Put 'er there, mates."

Again his hand is ignored.

"Christ, the whole fuckin' navy's sensitive. Wasn't that way in the Old Navy. Yeah, I'm an old salt myself. I got more time in the head than you got in the navy, sonny," he says to Larry. "In my day a man was a man, and now everybody's so goddamn sensitive. Jesus, I could go for a beer if you got one cold."

She puts the plates in front of the three at the table. She reaches into the refrigerator and gives Mr. Smith a can of beer. He pulls off the tab and takes a long swig. He sighs and belches up a fair amount of gas. With his little finger he digs lint out of his navel, exposed between the belt of his pants and the bottom of his dingy undershirt.

"S'cuse me, gents."

Meadows does not touch his food.

"So eat," says his mother.

"I'm not hungry," he says.

"Now look, Larry, don't pull that crap with me," says his mother. "You're not twelve anymore and neither am I. You'da thunk the navy would teach you."

"They taught me," he said, "to be afraid of crabs."

"Now what the hell is that remark?" says Mr. Smith. "Do I take that as a personal insult?"

Billy and Mule are smiling behind their hands.

"You could take him out back and kick his ass for that," whispers Billy to Mr. Smith.

"And you could butt out, skivvy waver," says Mr. Smith.

Billy signals with his hands: FOXTROT, UNIFORM, CHARLIE, KILO/break/YANKEE, OSCAR, UNIFORM.

Mrs. Meadows moves about the kitchen trying to restore order. "Boys, boys, boys, relax. Eat your breakfast and be nice."

"Here I am *trying* to be nice," says Mr. Smith. "If that kid don't want to chow, I can use it," he adds, beginning to reach.

Larry holds the sides of his plate.

"I want it now," he says and begins to dig in, as do the other two.

"I'll make you something," says Mrs. Meadows to Mr. Smith.

Mr. Smith pulls up his pants with a proprietary air and leans against the door frame, drinking his beer. The others eat.

"I ain't gonna let the world know, but you know how old I am, Larry. You gotta know that you and your young friends here ain't the only ones with needs. Everybody's got needs, even old farts like me and Mr. Smith."

Mr. Smith nods in assent.

"You think it's easy to be a woman what's used to it and have to wake up, go to work, and come home always by herself? I'm here to tell you it ain't. If I knowed you were coming home, I coulda made different plans. Made it nicer for you. But I think it's time you grew up, junior, and put your head into the world."

"He's such a sensitive kid, Leona," says Mr. Smith.

"You guys know," she says to Billy and Mule. "You're older, been around. Tell him about how people are, especially women. Tell him that women are just like men in that."

Billy and Mule do not look up from their plates.

"I don't have to apologize to anybody," says Mr. Smith. "I'm a veteran, regular navy."

"Would you have the manners to please shut up, Mr. Smith?" says Meadows' mother.

She dishes out another plateful and hands it to him, but Larry grabs it away from her. "I want some more," he says, and begins shoveling it in.

"Well, I'll be goddamned," says Mr. Smith.

"It's his house and he ain't home often," says Mrs. Meadows. "I'll make you some more." She turns to her son. "You turned into a peculiar kid in some ways, Larry."

"I think you spoiled him," says Mr. Smith. "Looks like a spoiled kid to me. I had five kids and my old lady raised them with the Bible in one hand and a switch in the other. They were raised right."

"You know, Mr. Smith," says Billy "what if you just go? That might make things easier."

"Listen to that, Leona. This guy blows in off some garbage scow somewhere and starts telling a veteran who's old enough to be his father where I can go. Did you get that shit, Leona?"

"Nobody has to go anywhere, just everybody eat and shut up. Christ, no wonder there's no peace in the world when . . ." she counts them up, ". . . five Americans can't get together in one lousy kitchen."

"Maybe he thinks that pop-gun scares me," says Mr. Smith. "When you been around as long as me, guns don't scare you. And you ain't got no jurisdiction over me no-way. I'm a civilian. Goddamn right."

Mrs. Meadows dishes out another plateful and hands it to Mr. Smith, but again Larry snatches it away.

"I'm still hungry," he says.

"I'll be go to hell!" shouts Mr. Smith. "He ain't even finished the last one."

In three quick forkfuls Larry finishes up one plate, slides it out of the way and starts on his third. Billy and Mule are still on their first plateful.

Mrs. Meadows looks at her son, mystified. "Larry, I don't think it's good for the system to bolt down six eggs and all those greasy potatoes."

"I'm hungry."

"Well, that's the last of the eggs. I'm sorry, Mr. Smith."

"I'm sorry, she says," says Mr. Smith. "I wanta tell you, Leona, this kid of yours and me ain't never gonna hit it off. Now I gotta go to some friggin' luncheonette and pay a buck for breakfast. I'll be go to hell."

"You should be," says Larry, with his mouth full.

Mr. Smith grabs his jacket from the couch and stomps out of the house. Larry looks a little ill because of the mess in his stomach.

"I must say, that was some performance," says his mother. "An Academy Award winner."

"I want to go back to the train," Larry says to Billy and Mule.

"I don't blame you. Mr. Smith can be a pain in the ass," says Mrs. Meadows. "But underneath it all, he's a real card. A great kidder. Stick around, Larry."

They put on their peacoats and walk toward the door.

"Good-bye Mother," says Larry.

She gives him half an embrace and a kiss on the cheek. He stands for it, but barely. As they leave the house, she calls after them, "I give you my word of honor—word of honor—I'm gonna write my congressman and have something done for you, Lar."

They overtake Mr. Smith, who says, "Well, if it ain't the little piggy and her keepers. Look at her, she's green around the gills."

Billy and Mule grab him and carry him into an alley. He struggles and says, "Cut the shit, mates. Us sailors got to stick together."

Billy shoves him against a brick wall. He cries, "Goddamn Cossacks!" Mule slaps him with a backhander.

"Sure, gang up on a defenseless old veteran," whimpers Mr. Smith. "What are you gonna do, murder me?"

"He's all yours, Larry," says Billy.

Larry faces him, makes a fist and raises it slightly. But he lets it drop. He cannot hit Mr. Smith. "I can't do it," says Larry.

Mr. Smith cringes against the wall. Billy pulls him by his shirt, spins him around and kicks him in the ass.

"Fly away, shitbird," he says.

Mule draws back and he too kicks Mr. Smith in the ass. Before he is out of the alley and running down the street, Larry is able to manage a swift kick. They look at each other.

"Would you say we got a generation gap here?" says Billy.

"Hellfire, I'm glad your momma don't have a chicken farm," says Mule. "You'd still be there, putting down those runny eggs."

Beginning with nothing louder than a hiccup, a tremendous round of laughter grows. They throw their arms around each other's shoulders and do an awkward little dance down the street, still laughing. Several people stop, bemused.

At the bus station, Larry throws up in the head and the other two avert their faces. Mule whispers to Billy, "A kid going to prison for eight should have more of a mother to say good-bye to, huh?"

"Nothing we can do about *that,*" says Billy.

"No, nothing about that."

They board the bus and in Philadelphia catch the train for New York. They skip lunch. Meadows goes down into himself. No one says a word about Mrs. Meadows or Mr. Smith. Billy doesn't read, Mule doesn't doze, and Larry doesn't look out the window.

"Well, what the hell," says Mule finally. "Let's go get some benies in the club car."

"Aye, aye, sir," says Billy and they all rise.

Mule walks ahead, followed by Meadows and Billy. Between two cars, Meadows shoves Mule forward savagely, elbows Billy behind him, and struggles with the outside door. It all happens in an instant, without warning, totally unexpected. Billy is on the floor, gasping for breath. Mule gets to Meadows as he is struggling with the door and grabs him by his jumper. He punches him hard in the stomach, and Meadows sinks to his knees. Billy gets to his feet and together they haul Meadows into the men's room and set him on a ledge between two washbasins.

Billy has to shout above the noise of the pounding wheels. "You trying to kill yourself or escape, which?"

"Both I guess," says Meadows.

"Both your sweet aunt's ass because one is the other. Why'd you figure they gave us these pieces, idiot? They're to shoot you with if you play rabbit."

Meadows looks at them in disbelief. "You'd *shoot* me if I ran?"

"Damn well told," says Mule breathing hard.

"And I'll tell you how it would be," says Billy. "They would give us a phony court-martial, fine us a dollar each, give us a couple of cartons of Salems and a set of confidential orders so none of your goddamn friends could get us. Believe me, lad, I know what I'm talking about. This is the *inside.* This train, these civilians—they're not real, they don't count, they're the *outside.* A dude can get killed here and on the outside they don't know, they don't care, it never even happened. And your old lady can write letters to your congressman until she owns the fucking post office. It don't mean nothing, do it, Mule?"

"It don't," says Mule.

"It's simple stuff, Larry. You gotta serve eight because the old man's old lady fucked over you, and we gotta take you there or we get keelhauled ourselves. Live with it, man. Don't fight it or you'll never smile again."

"None of my friends would get you," says Meadows. "I don't have any friends."

Billy covers his eyes with his hand and mutters, "Jesus Christ. Jesus Christ."

Mule is embarrassed and slightly ashamed. He leans against the washbasin and takes hold of a coat hook on the bulkhead.

"Look kid," says Billy gently. "*We'll* be your friends. If you let us. Don't make us be cops. We can be just three sailors together or we can be a prisoner and two pricks. It's up to you. I want you to promise us that you won't pull anything like that again. Give me your promise."

Meadows holds his hands together and looks between his knees at the floor. "Okay, I promise."

"Right," says Billy. "And I promise you that if you break your promise I'll kill you. I promise you that I won't even think about the value of life and the meaning of duty and the rest of that crap. I'll kill you 'cause there's no other selection."

"I'm sorry," Larry says, "I won't try it again. I was thinking about everything. Once I wanted to be a veterinarian. I thought that I could go to school on the G.I. Bill. I like animals."

"Listen, Meadows," says Mule, "live one day and then live another. Because the world changes every day. We know what eight years and a DD means today, but we don't know it'll always mean that. Like all those dudes in Canada now. You think they plan on staying there for good? Hell, no, man, they're just waiting for the world to change, one day at a time. Now let's get a drink. I ain't been so thirsty since I was a civilian in Lousyana."

"I'm sorry I did that and caused trouble," says Larry. "You guys pissed at me?"

"Hell, no," they say.

"It's all right you hit me, Mule," says Larry.

They file out of the men's room and continue on to the club car.

Five

THEY PUT THEIR .45'S AND arm bands into their AWOL bags and go to the Port Authority building because Billy says he likes the lockers there.

"Besides, this place has a smell to it and a kind of action about it," he says. "This is one of my favorite places in New York. Once I broke up a fight in here. Two guys I never even saw before. Gave me kind of a warm feeling."

"Yeah, I know what you mean," says Mule. "Once in a while it's nice to *stop* trouble."

"Had a shipmate, once," says Billy, "saw an ad in a magazine for a fountain pen that was actually a .22 gun. Wanted to get one and spend his liberties riding the subways, righting all wrongs and keeping evildoers in line. Took everything very personal, that boy."

"Too many wrongs to right," says Mule.

"Best you can do is hope to stay out of trouble yourself," says Larry.

"You tell 'em, kid, I stutter."

They go outside and past the delicatessen next door.

"This is a good place for a salami and Swiss on a roll with lots of mustard. On Sunday nights I used to get one here to eat on the sailors' bus back to Norfolk. Then I'd cover myself up with my peacoat and sleep all the way back to the ferry. That was before they put in the tunnel. Used to be a helluva long ride," says Billy.

"Did you spend much time here in New York?" asks Larry.

"You might say I lived here, as much as I lived anywhere on the beach."

"Could I ask where we're going?" says Larry.

"Right across the street."

They cross over to O'Brien's Inn. The windows are steamed over. Inside it is warm. They sit at the bar, their backs to the steam table laden with corned beef, pastrami, knackwurst, stuffed cabbage and a variety of other delicacies.

"I normally don't touch the hard stuff, but damn, look at those prices," says Billy.

Above the mirror behind the bar is a line of signs listing the kinds of whiskey that can be had, two shots for forty-five cents.

Meadows declines a shot, so they order three beers and two whiskeys. The bartender asks for Meadows' I.D., but this time there is no trouble since eighteen is the drinking age in New York.

"I could go for a knackwurst," says Mule.

"Later," says Billy. "I got a surprise for you."

"What's the plan of the day?" asks Mule.

"Well, hell, this is a democracy. How many vote we go to Boston tonight?"

No one moves.

"All right. How many vote we stay in New York tonight?"

Three hands are raised.

"That takes care of that."

"Where are we going to stay?" asks Larry.

"Well, let's see where we fall down," says Billy.

Billy and Mule have one more shot apiece but after that they stick to beer. The place is not busy and the bartender props his foot up on a case behind the bar and leans on his knee.

"So how's by you in the navy?"

"Same old crud."

"Yeah, well, it's like that everywhere."

"Ain't it a bitch?"

The bartender laughs. "I'd like you to explain one thing to me." He looks at each of them, indicating his willingness to take an answer from anyone. "Why are sailors so crazy?"

"Who the hell said they're crazy?"

"They are," says the bartender. "You guys probably are too for all I know. Never saw one that wasn't."

"We're all of us somebody's sons, you know."

"But crazy. Never saw one who wasn't."

"I guess you're gonna tell us about the one you saw that was, though, ain't you?" says Billy.

The bartender leans closer. "We got this bitch, she hangs around here, named Annie. A sailor comes in, she sits next to him and says, 'Hmm, hello, sailor. Sure, I'll have a drink. Tell me how long you got to serve this hitch?' 'Oh, I just shipped over six months ago.' Goodbye. She wants the one ready to ship over. Him she'll concentrate on long enough to get his shipping-over pay. The reenlistment money, you know?"

"Yeah, we know," says Mule. "She makes a good living, does she, like this?"

"A good living? We should all make such a good living like she makes. I can tell you she's made thirty-six thousand in this bar alone."

"C'mon."

"Word of honor. Listen I stood here one night and watched a sailor, twenty-two years old, count off four thousand dollars, *cash,* onto the bar and give it all to her. I saw that with my own eyes. For what? A squeeze on the dong under the bar? A few humps in the bed? Can you explain it to me what makes a sailor pay four thousand cash that he got for leave time and shipping over for a hole that's this wide and this far in?" The bartender measures off a bit of space between his forefinger and his thumb. "Crazy. No other explanation."

"That's the simple explanation," says Billy.

"You got another?"

"Well, you gotta understand the nature of a sailor," says Billy. "He ain't like other people."

"That much I know."

"Because he don't deal with the things that other people deal with. His job is on deep water. You only see sailors in this bar. If you saw 'em on deep water, you'd have yourself a different opinion of sailors."

"But four thousand dollars?"

"Don't mean a thing. When you get right down to it, there are only two things wrong with sailors: they don't have a single suspicious bone in their bodies and they're some of the loneliest people in the world. That's why when they come ashore they get very badly crapped on. 'Cause the people who live off them don't like them at all, but the sailors, poor dumb bastards, they don't know that, see?"

"I always give 'em a fair shake."

"Yeah but goddamn Annie, stay away from *her* fanny, huh?"

The bartender laughs. "You hit the needle on the eye there. You got a beer coming on me."

He gives them each a free beer and Billy cannot remember ever getting a beer for free in New York City before. It's that kind of place. He thinks that maybe it is a good omen. They have several more beers. The bar begins to fill up, and the bartender turns the TV set to the Sunday night movie. The sailors do not watch.

"Wisht I had a dog," says Larry.

"Huh?"

"Said I wisht I had a dog."

"What for?"

"For nothing. Just to have him so I could remember him."

"Didn't you ever have a dog?"

"Nope."

"How come?"

"Don't ask me. I just never did."

"What kinda dog you wish you had?" asks Mule.

"I don't know. Big old shaggy mutt, I guess."

Billy nervously yanks at the hair on the side of his head. "Larry?"

"Huh?"

"There ain't no way in hell we can get you a dog and travel the trains. It would be impossible."

"Who said anything about *getting* a dog? I just said I wisht I had one. It would be dumb to *get* a dog. How would we feed it and give it water and take it to the bathroom on the train? They wouldn't let a mutt *on* a train unless he was a seeing eye dog or something."

"That's what I just said. So the subject's closed, right?"

"Cats aren't as good," Larry says to Mule. "Can't rough-house them, and they're too damn independent. Want to be off by themselves all the time."

"How 'bout a nice little turtle?" says Mule.

"Look," says Billy, "I am the honcho, and we are *not getting a dog, we are not getting a cat,* and we sure as hell are not getting a fucking little *turtle!"*

"I don't see why you're getting so excited," says Larry.

"What's wrong with turtles?" asks Mule.

"Oh, I get it," says Billy. "You two bastards are trying to drive me bug-fug in the head, right?"

"Must am you're driving yourself bug-fug," says Mule.

"Must *am?"* says Billy.

Mule thinks for a moment and says, "Must be must am 'cause must is don't sound right, do it?"

Billy chokes and spits out his beer in a spray, catching the bartender on the elbow. "What is this, a geyser, I got here? This ain't Yellowstone National Park you know. Crazy!"

"You're beautiful, Mule," says Billy, "beautiful." Billy wipes his mouth then lifts his eyes and his palms to the heavens. "Here I am, A.J. Squaredaway, adrift without a paddle in the company of Admiral Kleptomania and William F. Buckley in blackface."

"I gotch your Admiral Kleptomania—dangling," says Larry.

Billy and Mule are stunned. "You see what you done now?" says Mule. "You messed over the kid's mind. He's starting to talk rotten just like you."

Billy is abject.

"They shoulda never done it, throwing a cherry in with hardened sailors like us," says Mule.

"I'm for washing out the little prick's mouth with lye soap," says Billy.

They grab him and pretend to be dragging him off to the men's room. He kicks and yells and says, "I'll never talk rotten again! Honest!"

"Cut the horseplay," says the bartender.

They let him go. Billy finishes his beer and says, "Okay, what about some chow?"

"I'm so hungry I could eat the ass end off a skunk," says Mule.

They leave O'Brien's and once in the street Billy cups his hands over his mouth and imitates the shrill piercing whistle of the bosun's pipe, going from a long low whistle to a piercing whine so high and long he loses it, then back to the low whistle, and finally to several quick short trills. A few passersby look over their shoulders. Holding his hand against his nose to approximate the sound of a ship's 1-MC intercom, he calls, "Now, all hands desiring to do so, lay down to the do-so locker and . . . do so."

They pile into a cab and Billy tells the driver, "Washington Square, my good man. Hang the expense."

After they disembark and pay the driver, Billy says, "You know, we're turning into drunken tourists. All we need are the cameras. Last night Washington, tonight the Village, spending money like a drunken tourist too."

"You've been here before, right?" asks Larry.

"Yeah, lotsa times, in the old days when everyone was a bohemian. Hell, when I was a kid I knew guys who were real Bohemians, I mean in the blood—Bohunks. Then all of a sudden I'm in Brooklyn and the skinny is go down to the Village where there's all these bohemian chicks, this was in what? Fifty-five, fifty-six.

The skinny was that bohemian chicks couldn't keep their hooks off soulful, lonely sailors. All you had to do was sit in some coffee shop and twist your white hat and some chick would come up and take you home with her. Well, maybe I wasn't soulful enough or lonely enough. But I do believe a dude could get laid for free pretty easy now with all this jailbait running around loose."

"If it's worth twenty years and a DD," says Mule.

"Go on!" says Larry.

"If she's under sixteen, you can get damn well up to twenty years."

"Even if she's the one who wants it?" asks Larry.

"Affirmative."

"Gee, that's only two years younger than I am. If they figure she's too young to do it how do they figure I'm old enough to do it, old enough to be in the navy even?"

"Different strokes for different folks," says Mule.

"Billy, is that true that if I did it with a girl who wasn't quite sixteen I could get twenty years?"

"You better bereave it. At hard labor."

"Jesus, a guy can sure get in trouble, huh?"

"Yeah, but don't you worry about it until you're ready, then you can decide what it's worth," says Billy.

"It ain't never gonna be worth twenty," says Mule.

"And a DD, you said," says Larry.

"For a hole this wide and this deep," says Billy, imitating the bartender.

He leads them across Washington Square to a cramped food stand with a narrow inner passage where up to four, maybe five, customers can escape the cold. He orders three Italian sausage sandwiches. They stare at the grill while the man takes three sausages from a tall pile and puts them on the hot part of the grill along with a good mound of onions and green peppers. They don't speak, they just watch the hissing food, feel the steamy warmth of the place, and inhale deeply.

The man takes the sausages, puts them into three fat Italian rolls and piles the onions and peppers on top. He gives them each a whack of salt from a dented tin salt shaker that hangs at the end of a thin chain. He smiles as he slides them over to the sailors. All three attack their sausages; they sigh and groan with delight.

"Now, I ask you," says Billy, "where do you expect to find a sandwich like this for half a buck?"

"I ain't jivin', I never ate anything so good," says Mule.

"I don't want to be a pig, but I know I'm going to hafta have another one of these," says Larry.

They each have another and leave with the good warm feel of grease in their mouths. Billy then leads them to another place "from the old days," The Ninth Circle, a cozy bar with sawdust and peanut shells on the floor. There is a massive barrel of peanuts just inside the door, and as Billy walks by he takes one of the plastic bowls sitting inside the barrel and scoops it full. They sit at a table and drink mugs of beer and eat peanuts, making a game of catching them in their mouths, tossing the shells on the floor.

"Gee, isn't this a great place?" says Larry.

"Yeah," says Mule, "and the great State of New York says even eighteen year olds and niggers can have a mug of beer."

"Seems to me the joint has calmed down," says Billy. "Used to be, there'd be some creep sitting at a table sketching, another writing poetry, a tableful of dudes arguing about the duty of the artist in urban life or some such crap, and by midnight you could expect an old-fashioned brawl. I miss the sounds of skulls cracking. Hell, I haven't been in a brawl in a coon's age."

"That's nice. That's fucking outstanding. I ain't heard that expression in a Polack's age," says Mule angrily.

"Mule, I'm sorry, but I can't change my whole damn vocabulary just like that."

"The way a person talks is the way a person thinks."

"Now that is absolutely untrue. Totally false. Guys say things because—well, they're just expressions. You know, the first thing that comes to mind. They don't mean anything by it. For instance, there's this nut I used to eat when I was a kid, we called it a nigger toe. It must have some other name, but I don't know what it is. Does that mean that all us kids were prejudiced because we used to eat nigger toes? I wouldn't go into a store today and say, gimme a bag of nigger toes. So what happens? I do without, I guess. What the hell do you call those nuts, anyway?"

Mule sulks and cracks open some peanuts and takes a long swig of beer.

"Well, hell, don't be all kinds of pissed off just because I'm ignorant," says Billy. "Set me straight. I'd still be calling 'em Negroes except I found out they wanted to be called blacks. Fine by me. So what do I call those kind of nuts?"

Mule takes another swig of beer and slams his mug down on the table. "Shitfire! I don't know. *We* used to call 'em niggertoes too!"

The three of them roar and beat the table with their fists. Billy orders another round of beers and they drink a toast to niggertoes.

By the time they leave The Ninth Circle they are drunk, Meadows more than the other two. They find themselves on a dark, narrow street, singing softly once again *"Whaddaya do with a drunken sailor . . ."* They stop in front of a building and Billy hushes the others. "Listen," he says.

"Yeah, I hear it too."

"Some kinda chanting," says Larry.

They keep still and listen to the sounds coming from the building. "What the hell is an Indiana dog?" asks Mule.

"A dog from Indiana, I guess. Why'd you wanna know?"

"Listen to 'em," says Mule. "They're saying Indiana dog over and over."

They listen carefully and sure enough, it sounds like *"Indiana dog, Indiana dog, Indiana dog, Indiana dog, Indiana dog, Indiana dog . . ."*

"That's the damnedest thing I ever heard," says Billy.

They walk up to the stoop and pasted to the door is a three-by-five card that reads:

NICHIREN SHOSHU OF AMERICA
USE SIDE ENTRANCE

"Must be some kinda New York strangie club," says Mule.

"Well let's take a look at the side entrance," says Billy.

The side entrance is on a walkway no more than four feet wide. Billy opens the door and they are in a spotless white vestibule. The sound of chanting is much louder now. On the floor are neat rows of shoes.

"Must be one of them Jap deals," says Mule.

"Either of you dudes have holes in your socks?" ask Billy as he unties his shoes.

"We should go," says Larry. "I have the feeling we're gonna get in trouble again."

"What do you mean, *again?* We ain't been in trouble *yet.*"

Meadows pauses to think about it and is surprised to realize that, technically, Billy is right. "Just a matter of time though," he says. "We weren't invited here."

"All they can do is kick us out if they don't want us," says Billy.

"These strangie groups, though, are usually open to the public," says Mule. "They like to make everybody as weird as them."

"How many strange groups you belong to?" asks Billy.

"Hell, I'm an old hand at this. I had a couple shipmates once were Unitarians."

They take off their shoes and place them carefully in one of the neat rows. They walk through a kitchen, following the sound of the chanting and come upon a living room where fifteen people are on their knees, in stocking feet, chanting to a scroll enshrined in a black altar. Two small candles burn on the altar and between them rises the smoke of incense from a ceramic holder. A bell and hammer sit on the floor next to the altar. As they chant, the worshippers vigorously rub strings of beads between their palms, and this action immediately reminds Mule of the way he handles dice. Behind the chanters against the wall, sit three other people, two men and a young girl, who watch but do not chant.

One of the chanters notices the three sailors and goes to them.

"Sorry to interrupt," says Billy. "We heard you from the outside and wandered in."

"You're very welcome. My name is Ron. Please sit with the other guests and we'll be with you in a moment."

They sit on the floor against the wall, and watch. To Billy, the chanting now sounds like, *"And on again and on again and on again and on again and on again . . .*" It has a soothing effect and Billy can feel himself almost drifting off. He feels suddenly less drunk but just as good. He does not shut his eyes for fear of falling asleep.

In deep tones, they give a new series of chants, slowly. Immediately afterward a young man jumps up and says, "Good evening!"

The others are all smiles and now answer, in unison: "Good evening!"

"Young Men's Division!" he says. "I've been on a Shakubuku!"

The men jump up and start swinging their right arms violently, as they all sing (to the tune of "I've Been Working on the Railroad"), *"I've been on a Shakubuku, all the live-long day! I've been on a Shakubuku just to start me on my way!"* The rest of the lyrics are unintelligible. As the song progresses, they clap their hands faster and faster so that neither the singing nor the swinging of the hands can keep up with the quickening pace. By the end of the song it has all crumbled into a confusion of sound.

The first young man remains standing after the others sit down and says again, "Good evening!"

He is answered in unison: "Good evening!"

He speaks over the heads of the chanters to the guests. "My name is Bob, and you're probably wondering what we're doing here, chanting and singing crazy songs." The chanters laugh and applaud. "This is a meeting of the Nichiren Shoshu of America. The best way to explain what it's all about is to hear from people who have been chanting and to hear what has happened to them because of it. Who's first?"

A dozen hands shoot up, like those of eager schoolchildren. Bob chooses one young man.

"Good evening!" he says.

The others respond again in unison.

"It's almost too much for words. I don't know how to tell you what Nam-Myoho-Renge-Kyo and the Gohonzon have done for me. The best way is to tell you what happened today. Did you ever wake up and see your mother at the door? She's got your suitcase on the floor and your toothbrush in her hand. 'Out,' she says. Well, that's exactly what happened to me today. Was I upset? I was smiling. I was happy. It makes you feel great inside. I threw my few things in my suitcase, took my toothbrush, and went outside. I started to chant right there on the sidewalk and in five minutes a car pulled up. It was a Buddhist! Well, to make a long story short, he gave me a lift to his job. Turns out he's been promoted and now I have his old job. I've got a new place to live. Everything's great!"

There is a long, loud round of applause.

A teenybopper gets up now and almost bounces as she talks, waving her hands in the air. "A year ago," she says, "I was like everybody else—half-dead. I was antisocial, apathetic. I was in a drug bag. I was pom . . . prom . . . 1 was fooling around a lot. A year ago I'd never dream of standing up and talking like this in front of people. Then I started chanting and everything changed. I wanted to *do* things. Well, I wanted a flute real bad and my cousin knew a guy and was going to get one for me. I really chanted for it. I just chanted and chanted. Well, the guy didn't have the flute any more and my cousin got a clarinet for me instead. I *love* that clarinet! I never wanted a flute in the first place. Now I'm in the *Drum and Fife Corps!* If you knew me a year ago, you'd know what a *fantastic* thing this is—*me* in the Drum and Fife Corps!"

She sits down amid the applause and gives the floor to an effeminate young man who stands up and says, "I came to New York from California. I was at the end of my rope. I weighed over two hundred pounds, I was sleeping twelve hours a day, I was a royal mess. The first person I met in New York was a girl who brought me to a meeting like this. I thought they were all nuts!" (Laughter.) "Later, I went to this girl's apartment and used her Gohonzon. Boy, was I skeptical! I was going to put the Gohonzon to a real test. There was a poster of Peter Fonda on her wall, the one where he's on this magnificent chopper, and I said, 'O.K. if the Gohonzon is so hot, I want to meet Peter Fonda.' She said, 'Chant for it and see what happens.' So I chanted for twenty minutes just to test it. I walked out of her apartment, went down the street, and at the intersection I was hit by a cab. Who was the passenger? You guessed it—Peter Fonda! It blew my mind. I couldn't believe it. What's more, I had a simple fracture of the leg and made a pretty nice settlement. That was a year ago and I've been chanting ever since. I've lost thirty-five pounds, I only need about five hours of sleep a night, my life has become beautiful. I can't explain it. It just works. If throwing avocados against the wall worked as well as Gohonzon, I would throw avocados against the wall."

Larry whispers to Billy, "What's avocados?"

"A fruit kinda like, grows in California."

"Oh."

There is another rousing round of applause for this testimonial.

Bob stands up again and says, "Everybody in this room could tell you about fantastic material, physical, and spiritual gains through chanting. We could talk about theory but it would only be a waste of time. Just believe me when I tell you that all your desires will be realized through chanting. But what's more important is that you'll feel wonderful inside. So how about it? Do you want to try it? What about the navy?"

They exchange looks and Billy speaks for them. "Well, I'll tell you. These three sailors here could use a certain desire or two. You don't know the half of it."

"Are you willing to try?"

"Hell's bells, we're sailors. We'll try anything once."

Everyone applauds and cheers as though this is the most original and total statement of commitment.

The meeting ends with an out-of-tempo rendition of "Those Were the Days, My Friend," with slightly altered lyrics. Bob approaches them afterward and says, "The first thing you've got to do is get your Gohonzon."

"What's a Gohonzon?" says Larry.

"It's the scroll you chant to. It represents infinite power."

"Well, where do we get one?" asks Billy.

"You can't until next week, I'm afraid, at the regular temple ceremony."

"That shoots it," says Billy. "We're leaving New York in just a few hours."

"Damn," says Bob, "that's too bad."

"The way our luck is running, wouldn't make much difference."

"That's where you're wrong. Chanting works. Listen, even though you don't have your Gohonzons or your beads, chant anyway. Whenever you get the chance, wherever you are. Just chant the words Nam-Myoho-Renge-Kyo over and over again. Things will start to happen. Good things."

"Shitfire," says Mule, "we'll give 'er a shot or two just to try it out."

They leave the house and continue walking.

"Packa strangies if you ask me," says Mule.

"Damn happy-looking, though, weren't they?" says Billy.

"Sure were," says Larry.

The three of them begin chanting, "*Nam-Myoho-Renge-Kyo, Nam-Myoho-Renge-Kyo . . .*"

"I ain't sure this will replace 'Whaddaya Do with a Drunken Sailor?'" says Billy. "It's a bit repetitious."

"It's kinda fun, though, isn't it?" says Larry.

"But we gotta decide on what we want to chant *for*," says Billy.

"How 'bout that Larry gets sprung from Portsmouth?"

"I'm for that," says Larry.

"That was my idea too," says Billy, "but I think we should try it out on something small and quick first so we can see if it works before we waste a lot of time going for the big one."

"Any ideas?" says Mule.

"What about that we all get laid?"

"I don't think that's a fit desire to chant for," says Larry. "It shows a lack of respect."

"Larry, kid, you're too good to believe sometimes," says Billy.

"Let's make it nice and simple," says Mule. "Let's chant that a beautiful lady picks us up and takes us to her house for the night and just let it go at that."

"That sounds like a reasonable test," says Billy.

"Agreed," says Larry.

And so they continue down the street chanting for their beautiful lady.

They stop at Café Romeo and find a corner to themselves. Their uniforms capture momentary attention from the regulars but then they go back to their chess games and quiet discussions. The waitress comes and Billy orders a cappuccino.

"What's a cappuccino?" asks Larry.

"Italian coffee with whipped cream and nutmeg on the top."

"That sounds okay. One for me too."

"Me, too," says Mule.

As they wait, they chant softly, almost inaudibly. They have their heads on their hands and stare at the table. Mule sees a shadow move next to him. He raises his head and sees what could easily qualify as a beautiful lady. He nudges Billy with his knee. Billy looks up, and Larry goes on chanting for a few seconds before he realizes he is doing it alone. The girl stands with her hands on her hips, a leather bag hanging from her shoulder. She says, "Like they say, you can expect to find anything in the Village."

"Hello, Charlotte," says Billy.

"Billy."

"Meet my friends. Mule Mulhall and Larry Meadows."

Larry rises and glares at Mule, who then rises. Even Billy lifts himself a few inches from his chair and says, "Sit down, Charlotte. Can we order you something?"

"No thanks. See you made first class. Coming up in the world." She sits down.

"Time in and a clean record."

"Which means you've never been caught."

"That's what clean records are all about, not getting caught."

The girl brings the cappuccino. Larry takes a quick sip and burns his lip. He waves his hand in front of his lips to cool them.

"The cold whipped cream'll fake you out every time," says Billy.

"Mind if I ask what you were doing?" asks Charlotte.

"Chanting," says Larry. "We just started."

"What do you mean, chanting?"

"Like the Buddhists," says Larry.

"Like *religious* chanting?"

"Well, yeah."

"Billy, you certainly have changed." She speaks to the others. "Billy almost found religion several years ago. He was about to join until he found out that the Trinity wasn't three in bed."

A tableful of people get up to leave and call out, "Charlotte, we're going."

"Night all," she calls back. "See you tomorrow."

"Don't get carried away with patriotism," one of them warns and then adds as he leaves, "We'll always know where to find Charlotte. Just keep turning right."

In answer, Charlotte flashes a V-sign.

"Still run with a packa shits, huh?" says Billy.

"Do you really feel you have the right to criticize my choice of friends?"

"Guess so. I did it anyway."

Again she speaks to the others. "Present company excluded, but Billy has in his history the oddest collection of friends one person could possibly assemble."

Mule says, "Miss, excuse me, but who *are* you? I don't figure Billy'll ever tell."

"I used to be, if you'll excuse the expression, Mrs. Bad-Ass."

Mule and Larry are dumbfounded.

"May be still, for all I know," says Billy.

"Don't get your hopes up."

"Married now, Charlotte?"

"Thank you, no."

"Well, what have you been doing with yourself?"

"I have an apartment here in the Village, I have the grooviest job, I have lots of friends."

"Still secretarying?"

"Yes, but now I'm at Columbia Records."

She waits for a moment but there is no reaction. Larry finally says, "You mean like record albums? I mean like, what do you do? Is it in a recording studio or something?"

"I'm in the business offices but I can go to the studios anytime I want to, and I get to meet most of the stars when they come into the office. Just last Friday I had a long conversation on the phone with Johnny Mathis."

"Heard he's a fag," says Billy.

"That's a rotten thing to say about someone you never met."

"Nothing wrong with being a fag. Just wouldn't want one marrying my brother," says Billy.

"Every Tom, Dick, and Harry thinks he can say anything he wants to about a person as long as that person is a celebrity," says Charlotte.

"You should hear how he talks about George Washington," says Larry.

Charlotte turns to Larry and raises an eyebrow. Then she turns back to Billy and says, "It's one of your typical rotten things to say about civilized people. You're rather rotten inside, Billy."

"Either that or I'm not."

"What's more, you're exasperating. This is like going back into a nightmare but now at least you're sure it's not real life. You can wake up and walk away from it."

"You're being dramatic, Char. We had some good times."

"Sure we did, but that's not a marriage, some good times."

"I'm sorry about all that, Char, but you knew I was a lifer in the navy."

"Hey, man, would you like it if Larry and me took a walk around the block?" asks Mule.

"Stay," says Charlotte. "Billy and I have been split for over four years. If the talk gets personal, at least it's objective and without emotion."

"How long were you married?" asks Larry.

"That's relative," says Charlotte.

"Huh?"

"Married people are people living together. For us that was six months, in two installments. The first three months right after we were married, then nine months he was in the Med. Then three months together again, him, me, and his wacky friends, and then another nine months in the Med. So you might say we were married two years, but I wouldn't say so."

"Sorry, Char," says Billy.

"Yes, I know. You don't make the rules, you just follow them."

"Something like that."

"At least you could have been unhappy about it."

"I was unhappy to leave you."

"But not to be getting underway, playing with your flags and toys and stupid war games."

"Don't poke fun at something you don't understand."

"There's really no point in rehashing it, is there? What's done is done."

"That's the spirit. Let me buy you a drink, old girl."

"Just coffee at the Romeo and I'm over-coffeed already. Thanks." They sit for a moment in silence. Billy sips his cappuccino. Mule and Larry have already finished theirs.

"How's the navy now?" she asks.

"Rocks and shoals, port and starboard, same old stuff."

"What are you doing in the city? Are you out at Brooklyn again?"

"No. No, we're not."

"Well, where are you?"

"In transit, in Norfolk, waiting for permanent orders."

"Just here for weekend liberty?"

"Not exactly."

"Then what in the hell *are* you doing here?"

Larry lowers his head.

"Don't get excited, Charlotte. We're only stopping over on the way to Boston. Gonna get a plate of beans there."

Charlotte sighs. "You're a pretty impossible guy, Billy Bad-Ass."

"Hey, you're either pretty or you're impossible, one. Which for me?"

"Impossible," says Charlotte.

"You think so? You should get to meet this Meadows kid. He's from another planet. Or this Mule. He's one of them black militants you've been hearing so much about."

"Really?" says Charlotte. "I'm very sympathetic to the black cause and support what they're doing."

Mule shakes his head diffidently and gives a little wave of his hand. "Billy's only making a joke. I ain't as black-militant as all that."

"Well, you should be. I'm sure the navy of all places deserves some organized resistance on the part of black sailors."

"Charlotte," says Billy, "you don't know anything about the navy and you don't know anything about black sailors."

"Is that your way of telling me to shut up?"

"That's my way of telling you you don't know anything about the navy and you don't know anything about black sailors."

"Well, I'll shut up anyway. Nice meeting you two," she says to Mule and Larry. "And it was good to see you again, Billy. Souvenirs. See you later, alligator."

She rises to go, but Billy touches her arm with the tips of three fingers and she sits down again.

"What?" she says.

"Charlotte, we got no place to flop tonight. Could you give us a floor?"

"I don't think so."

"We'll have to go to one of those movies on Forty-second Street for the night then."

"With the rest of the misfits. Might turn out to be a wonderful reunion for you."

"Wish you wouldn't hate people for all the wrong reasons."

"I don't hate you."

"So let us flop."

"I'll give you the money for the movies."

"Dammit, Charlotte, we need a shower. We've been transiting around all the damn day."

"You shipped over for it."

"That don't mean I gotta die of B.O."

Charlotte laughs in spite of herself and is unhappy for blowing her cool.

"You could go to the Y," she says.

"You can say that 'cause you've never been to the Y."

"Excuse my inexperience."

"*That* we don't worry about, but you've never been to the Y."

"Sorry."

Billy takes a long minute to adjust his neckerchief.

"I want you to listen to me, Charlotte. Mule and I are what you call chasers. We're taking Larry to the naval prison at Portsmouth."

"That's in New Hampshire," says Larry.

"He's going in for eight years and we're trying to stretch the trip there. So far it hasn't been so damn happy, to make a long story short."

At the mention of eight years in prison, Charlotte puts her hand over her mouth in astonishment. She reaches over and puts a hand on Larry's shoulder.

"I'm sorry. Of course you can sleep on my floor."

They leave the café and walk the several blocks to her apartment. Snow begins to drift down in large leafy flakes.

"Snowing again," says Larry.

"Won't stick, though," says Mule. "Ain't cold enough."

Her apartment opens onto the kitchen, which is adjacent to the bathroom. Beyond the kitchen is a bedroom, and to the left of it a living room distinguished by an expensive stereo and an overpowering collection of records.

"Most of them I got for nothing or next to it. Since I work in the business."

She slides a few records out of their jackets and stacks them on the spindle. She flips a switch and in a few seconds Aretha Franklin's voice fills the room. She turns down the volume.

"Throw your hats and jackets anywhere. When I'm alone I like it loud. How else to listen to Aretha Franklin? So much soul there. I met her once."

"She forgot the words to 'The Star-Spangled Banner,'" says Billy.

"Will you *stop* it?"

"Well, she did. If you saw the convention on TV, you'd know."

"What the hell were *you* doing watching a political convention?"

"Just because I am a sailor doesn't mean I don't know what's going on."

"She's a good singer anyway, isn't she, Mule?" says Charlotte.

"Oh, sure, one of the best," says Mule quickly.

"So there, sit down and shut up. What do you want to drink? Are you still a wino, Billy?"

"I do enjoy a taste of the grape from time to time—for the digestion."

Charlotte pours out four long-stemmed glassfuls and brings them to the living room on a tray along with the bottle.

"Isn't this fancy?" says Billy. "Real wine glasses. What'd you do with all the peanut butter and jelly glasses, Char?" He lifts the glass and says, "Here's to our women and our horses and those who mount 'em."

They all drink and settle down, Mule and Larry on the sofa, Charlotte and Billy on the floor. Billy looks at the bottle. "*Chenin Blanc.* Not bad. You sure you're still a secretary?"

"Don't be a wise-ass."

They listen to the music and have another glass of wine.

"Excuse me if I'm being gauche, Larry, but what did a kid like you do to deserve eight years?" asks Charlotte.

"What does gauche mean?" asks Larry.

"Lacking in social graces," says Billy. "A shitbird."

"Oh."

"So what did you do? If you don't mind talking about it."

"Oh, that, well, I'm afraid I stole forty dollars outa the commissary store, in a polio box thing."

"Forty dollars? Without a gun or anything?"

"The thing is," says Mule, "Larry's mind is messed up. He's got a mental sickness. They call it kleptomania."

"Then he should have treatment. It's not his fault."

"What he *should* have and what he's *going* to have are two different things," says Billy. "There's a lot you don't know about, like the old man's old lady having a hard-on for him."

"The old heave-ho," says Mule.

"And you two brutes are just going to drag him to prison and drop him there?"

"In the first case," says Billy, "we ain't brutes, we're just sailors. And in the second case we ain't going to exactly *drag* him there and in the second case also we ain't gonna exactly *drop* him there."

"You are brutes, you know that?"

"No, they ain't," says Larry. "They're all right."

"Do you think we'd do it if we had a selection?" says Billy.

"The original Pavlov dog," says Charlotte.

"What's that?" asks Larry.

"Don't ask so many questions," says Billy.

"Well how'm I ever going to learn anything?"

"What I'm saying is that a bell rings and your two *friends* here jump."

Larry doesn't know what she's talking about.

"I'm not too wild about your analysis of the situation, Char baby," says Billy.

"You're Judas goats, both of you."

"What's a Judas goat?" asks Larry inevitably.

Billy bawls, "I'm gonna go outa my son-of-a-bitchin' mind!"

"I don't doubt that," says Charlotte. "Don't look for any sympathy from me when you do."

"Don't be so rough on us," says Mule. "There's a matter of asses involved here."

"Your ass or his ass, right?" says Charlotte.

"On the button," says Mule.

"That's the trouble with this whole damn society, but no place is it as maniacal as in your beloved US Navy."

"Since when are you so worried about this whole damn society, Char?" asks Billy. "It used to be your waistline."

"You can be as funny as you want. The only reason you don't give a damn about the world is that you're not living in it."

"You sure are treating me discourteously."

"Let him go, Billy. Mule?"

"Huh?"

"Let him go. You can say he gave you the slip. You could go to Canada, Larry."

"What for?" asks Larry.

"For freedom. What else? You won't be alone up there."

"I don't want to go to Canada. I'm from New Jersey."

"Don't you want to be free?"

"Sure."

"But you don't want to go to Canada?"

"Huh-uh."

"Would you run if Billy and Mule let you?"

"Maybe, but they won't let me, and I gave 'em my word I wouldn't. They'd get in a lotta trouble if I did."

"A matter of asses," says Charlotte.

"I hate to break up this philosophizing about the abstracts, but do you have another bottle of wine, Charlotte?"

"No. That was the last. There's a liquor store on the corner." The tone of her voice has the edge of irritation and defeat to it.

"I suppose you want some more *Chenin Blanc*, huh?"

"I don't care," she says.

"I'm partial to Sly Fox myself, the wine that killed Norfolk, Virginia."

"Get whatever you want."

"I guess they wouldn't have it here in the big city, though."

"Do you want us to go with you?" asks Larry.

"No, you two sit here and amuse old Charlotte."

Billy puts on his peacoat and leaves.

Larry breaks a few minutes' silence when he says to Charlotte, "I hope you're not mad at us."

"I should butt out. You're three grown men, you should make your own decisions."

"Well, when it comes to that, old Billy Bad-Ass is the honcho," says Larry. "That means he's the man in command."

"You're fond of Billy, aren't you?"

"Oh, he's a great guy. He ain't a mean bastard like the MAA said. MAA's lie a lot."

"You too, Mule?"

"Huh?"

"You like Billy?"

"He's a good old partner."

"Everybody likes good old Billy Bad-Ass," says Charlotte. "Funny isn't it?"

"I'm sorry you two couldn't hit it off together," says Larry. "You really make a nice-looking couple. But that's the way it happens sometimes, I guess."

"How long have you two known each other?"

"Let's see," says Larry. "Two days? Yeah, two days."

Charlotte is astounded. "And you, Mule?"

"Met him yesterday morning."

"Mule knows him longer than me. I met him yesterday afternoon."

"Then you don't know anything about him."

"You get to know a guy fast in the navy," says Mule.

"Do you realize he's a fake?"

"Whaddaya mean?" asks Mule.

"This tough talk and all that ungrammatical crap. He's read enough to speak flawless English if he wanted to."

"He's one smart honcho, that's for sure."

"He could make something of himself if he got out of the stupid navy."

"But he *likes* it," says Mule.

"Can you beat that? He really *does*," says Charlotte. "Poor dumb Polack."

"That don't make him a fake," says Mule.

"You can't ever be sure what he's thinking"

"He never lied to me," says Mule.

"In all the two days you've known him."

"Right."

"He's a brute. You both are. On the outside. And maybe that's where it really counts."

"No, we ain't."

"Do you want to know what he said to me once when I was bitchy, right after we made love?"

"Maybe you shouldn't tell us," says Larry.

"He said that making love to me was like sticking his prick out of the window and fucking the world."

Larry turns crimson. Mule chuckles and covers his mouth with the back of his hand.

"He's got a way with words. Perhaps you've noticed," says Charlotte.

Mule chuckles again.

"You're brutes."

"Well, you said you were a bitch," says Mule.

"You'd be bitchy too."

There is a knock on the door. "Who is it?" calls Charlotte.

"It's the landlord and I want my rent," says Billy from the other side of the door. She lets him in.

"Here it is. *Chenin Blanc*, what the hell, I work for a living too. Work for the president of the United States. Was at his place just last night."

"Excuse me," says Charlotte and goes into the bedroom. Billy goes into the living room with a bottle of wine in each hand. "What's up her ass?"

"Damned if I know," says Mule. "We were talking about you and all of a sudden she got kinda depressed."

"Well, that'll do it every time. She'll be all right."

He fills their glasses and sits on the floor. He lights a cigarette. Charlotte comes back with a Baggie in one hand and some strawberry paper in the other. "Grass, anybody?"

"I'll be damned, Char," says Billy. "I leave you for a few years and you turn into a pothead."

"It beats what all that wine is doing to your liver," she says.

"I don't drink for effect, I drink for *taste*. You'll notice I don't chew gum or eat candy."

"Bully for you. Mule? Larry?"

"I'm in enough trouble as it is," says Larry.

She rolls a joint, twists each end, and gives the length of it a second run across the tip of her tongue. After several draws, she produces a sequined roach clip for the rest of the joint. "All right. So much the more for me," she says.

"I'll tell you, Charlotte," says Billy, "the last time I smoked the stuff I went half nuts sexually, you know? How about we talk about it in bed?"

"All *four* of us?" she says.

Billy looks at the other two. "I don't mind if they don't."

"I bet you don't, you freaky swab jockey. Forget it. This isn't one of your ports and I'm not one of your girls."

"That myth," says Billy.

Larry has been watching her with fascination. "Feel anything yet?" he asks.

Charlotte laughs a benign laugh and the tension drains from her. "You really ought to let him go," she says. She laughs again and says, "No, Larry. I'm not going to dance naked." The idea tickles her and she breaks into a fit of giggling.

"There was lots of that stuff around Camden when I was in school and all the kids were smoking it, even in the heads, you know, between classes, but I was always too scared to try it. I had that trouble, like I told you, with the cops. Gee, I missed out on a lot, when you look at it. I wonder what the craze will be in the seventies."

"If you want to try a joint, go ahead," says Billy.

"It's all right with you?"

"Sure, what the hell."

"Well, maybe later I will—just to say I tried it. I'm flying high enough on beer and wine. I never drank so much in my life as these past two days."

Charlotte finishes the roach and puts away her paraphernalia. She goes into the bathroom. When she comes back into the living room, Larry is standing by the bookcase. He picks up a wooden instrument and asks, "What's this, Charlotte?"

"It's a shepherd's pipe."

The instrument is about a foot long with two reeds, side by side. The shaft parts into two columns halfway down. There are four finger holes on one column, three on the other. The pipe is carved with a pattern of squares and triangles. "Go ahead, try it," says Charlotte.

Larry blows into it and taps his finger over the holes. The discordant notes break and squeak. He does a Pied Piper dance as he plays. Charlotte giggles again and Mule and Billy smile.

"With that I think I'm ready to crash," says Charlotte. She brings out three blankets and drops them on the floor. "These are all the blankets I have. If you get cold during the night you can use your peacoats. Use the pillows from the sofa. I laid out towels for you in the bathroom."

"You're a good old egg," says Billy.

"Hey!" says Larry, and slaps himself on the forehead. "It works! The chanting really works! Oh, boy, am I going to get to work!"

"What's he raving about?" asks Charlotte.

"I told you," says Billy. "He's from another planet, this kid."

"Good night," says Charlotte. "See you all in the morning."

They wish her good night and take turns in the shower. They put on their day-old skivvies, wrap themselves in their blankets and stretch out on the floor. Larry says, "Hey, one of us could sleep on the couch, you know."

"Please, please, please," says Billy. "Let's not start that again."

"I was just saying."

"Knock it off and go to sleep."

"Okay, Billy."

Mule wakes up during the night. He sees that Billy is not in his blanket and there is no light on in the bathroom. He smiles, turns over, and goes back to sleep.

It is eight-thirty in the morning. Billy is fully dressed, standing between the kitchen and the living room with a cup of coffee in hand. He presses his other hand against his nose and imitates the bosun's pipe. "Now reveille, reveille, reveille!" he shouts. "Drop your cocks and grab your socks! Reveille!"

Larry groans and puts his hands to his temples. "Oh, I feel awful," he moans. "Not so loud, Billy."

"Toughen up, kid, have a drink. It'll square you away."

"God, don't mention it. I'm never gonna drink again."

"You remind me of myself when I was your age. Only I was better-looking."

Mule snorts and pulls the blanket over his head. Billy goes about getting two more cups of coffee. Charlotte's voice can be heard from the bedroom. "Hello, Grace? This is Charlotte. I'm going to be late today. No, I just spent the night with three sailors and it's going to take me a while to pull myself together. Would I lie to you? When he comes in tell him I called and I'll be a little late, that's all. Thanks, Grace. See you."

Billy carries two cups into the living room. He gives Mule a kick and puts the cup on the floor in front of him. A shaky hand snakes out from under the blanket and latches on to it. Then a sad-eyed face emerges. He wraps the blanket around himself and sits Indian-style drinking his coffee. Larry is sitting on the sofa and accepts the coffee sullenly.

"Get yourselves squared away, candy-asses. I'm going down to Port Authority for the bags."

"What for?" asks Larry.

"Charlotte says it's all right for us to spend another night here."

"Great, but what about Portsmouth?"

"Look, they always give you more time than you need on a detail like this. No one at Portsmouth is gonna sweat why it took us so long as long as we're there before the deadline."

"Great."

"What about you, Mule?"

Without looking up, Mule gives the thumbs-up sign.

"Okay, see you in a little bit."

Charlotte has gone to her job at Columbia Records before Billy returns. She mentions in parting that there's a good chance she will meet Tony Bennett this day. When Billy returns, they shave and put on fresh skivvies. They spend the day bumming around the cold streets of New York. At Grant's on Times Square they each have a beer and a hot dog that crackles as they chew it. Billy and Mule buy Larry an I.D. bracelet for one ninety-eight and have engraved on it: L. MEADOWS. "There's still room for rank if you want me to put it," says the engraver.

"No, I don't think so," says Larry.

"Wait a minute," says Billy. "I think it's time you make your rate."

Larry whispers to Billy, "C'mon, they busted me to E-l, you know that."

"So what? Right now we're in a navy of three. Pick a rate, any rate. I'm the honcho and I can promote you if I want to. What'll it be?"

"Chief signalman?"

"Done! Okay, partner, engrave in there after the name: SMC."

Mule fastens the clip and stands back to admire it.

"Very sexy," he says. "Chicks love to see you wearing doodads like that."

"What I should do is get those red dragons sewn inside my cuffs," says Larry.

"Negative. They're not regulation, and we're regulation sailors right down to the skivvies."

"They're okay as long as you don't turn up your sleeves so people can see 'em," says Larry.

"So what's the point of having the damn things?"

"I don't know. I guess it is kind of dumb, ain't it?"

"For an SMC, sure."

"Hey! I outrank you dudes."

Larry barks orders at them, in imitation of irascible old SMC's. Mule and Billy snap to and answer sharply, "Aye, aye, chief."

He orders a landing party to proceed to the Village and commandeer half a dozen Italian sausage sandwiches. They go to the same stand and the man recognizes them from the night before. He conveys his respect for such healthy appetites as they wolf down two apiece.

They loaf around until six o'clock, when they go back to Charlotte's and take her for a lobster dinner at McGinnis's. Larry can remember having had only one other lobster tail in his life. He is ecstatic. "But do we have enough chits for all of this? It's damned expensive. I feel like a moocher, I don't have a dime."

"We're fat cats," says Mule.

They go to Rockefeller Center and watch the skaters. They learn that of the four of them, Charlotte is the only one who's ever been on ice skates.

"Someday I'm gonna give that a try. I got pretty good balance and coordination from playing basketball. I bet I could do that," says Larry.

They go to Radio City Music Hall and see a movie plus a stage show. The movie is a dog, but Larry likes it because Natalie Wood is in it and he says during the intermission that Charlotte looks a lot like Natalie Wood. It pleases her to hear that, because people have said it before. Mule and Billy ogle the Rockettes, and once outside make silly remarks about smorgasbord. Larry is more impressed with the man who played the organ. "That's the biggest organ I ever saw in my life," he says. Billy and Mule laugh and carry on some more about the Rockettes. Charlotte gives the two of them a punch in the stomach, hurting her hand on a button on Mule's peacoat. "Ouch, that went right through the glove," she says.

They go back to the apartment and teach Larry how to smoke grass.

"Ain't exactly Salems, is it?" he says. "Burns the hell out of the throat."

"When it's legal they'll filter and cool it," says Charlotte.

"Smells like hay," says Larry. "Kinda pleasant."

Afterward Larry's throat is very dry and he sips a Coke with ice. "Doesn't seem to have much effect on me except to make me dry as hell." But, in a few moments he hogs the conversation and everything he says strikes him as brilliantly funny. At one point he asks Charlotte if she met Tony Bennett that day.

"No. He didn't come in today," she says. "Maybe tomorrow."

"Too bad. Would have been nice for the folks back home."

This seems to him to be the most clever thing ever uttered and he rolls on the floor, giggling almost girlishly. The only noticeable effect on Mule and Billy is that Mule's eyes clear up and the wrinkles on Billy's forehead melt away.

It is not quite midnight when Charlotte makes her exit and they bundle up in their blankets and go to sleep.

Billy is not so cheerful in the morning as he was the day before. He gives them each a gentle shake and says, "Let's go. It was all right while it lasted. Now there's a train."

After they have dressed, Charlotte joins them for coffee. She wears a bathrobe and holds her left arm across her waist. She watches them put their few things together. They put on their peacoats and seem ready to go, but Mule and Billy dig into their AWOL bags and pull out their SP bands. They help each other to secure them on their arms.

"What's this?" asks Charlotte.

They do not answer. They remove the .45's from the bags and bring the guard belts around their waists.

"What the hell is this?"

"We're supposed to wear these goddamn things, Charlotte, when we're traveling," says Billy. "What if we kept them in the bags and then lost the bags somewhere? It'd be our asses."

"Oh, this is awful," says Charlotte.

"I don't mind," says Larry.

"We're supposed to have him in handcuffs too," says Mule, "but enough is enough."

"You really are brutes."

"Please, Charlotte."

"Okay, you're ready to go, so go," she says.

"So long, old girl, many thanks," says Billy.

"Yeah," says Mule. "Thanks a lot."

"I really had a time to remember, marijuana and everything," says Larry. "But most of all I'll remember meeting you. You're a nice person."

Swiftly she puts her arms around his neck and kisses him on the cheek. Then she steps backward to the wall and leans against it. Larry blushes.

"Okay," says Billy. "Let's go. See you, Char."

They leave the apartment and go downstairs to the street. They decide on the convenience and expense of a cab.

"Wait a minute," says Billy. "I forgot something."

He pushes the doorbell.

"What?" asks Mule.

"Something."

The buzzer sounds and he opens the door. He takes the steps two at a time. Charlotte is standing in the hall.

"Look, Charlotte you've been a peach, and I really mean that. The kid is walking on air. It's gonna be a little easier now."

"But?"

"But could you lend me twenty bucks?"

"Twenty bucks! Isn't this where I came in?"

"It's not for me, dammit. The kid doesn't have any money, you heard him. We want to show him a good time in Boston, but I'm afraid we're gonna run outa money. If we got it left over on the return trip, I'll stop by and pay you back."

She goes to her purse and returns with twenty-five.

"I feel sorry for him," she says.

"I promise I'll stop on the return trip, and if we still have it, we'll give it back."

"You know the address. You could mail it from Norfolk."

"But, dammit, I *want* to stop."

"Why?"

"Charlotte, don't bust my hump. I want to see you again. I've still got something for you, and I could tell these past two nights you've still got something for me."

"I can't very well deny it, can I?"

"Whaddaya think, Char? A chance?"

"There's always a chance. See me when you get your discharge. Ha, ha," she says mirthlessly.

"Well, that's what I was thinking."

"You serious?"

"It's hard not to do an awful lot of thinking—the way things are."

"What, in ten years? Is that what you have left?"

"Well, it's hard to talk about it because I'm still thinking, and a lot has been happening around here."

"You going to get out?"

"Don't make me say anything now, Char, this is rough."

"I'll be here, Billy. You think it out. It's one of those capital *D* decisions for you, and I understand that. I'm not kidding when I say I'll be here."

"Maybe I'll know for sure when we come back through, and that'll be in only a few days."

"You come here. The super will have the key."

"Something surer than hell is gonna give. I can feel it in my fingers."

"The super will have the key."

He pulls her to him and kisses her and feels inside of him a frightening tenderness, a disarming tenderness.

As the train pulls out of the station, Larry says, “I’ve been in New York before but never like this. I could go for living every day of my life like this, I think.”

“Yeah,” says Billy, “and the people in hell could go for ice water, they think.”

They talk about the good Italian sausages and the Rockettes and Charlotte’s kindness. Larry turns his face toward the window. His eyes are wet and his body heaves a little.

“What’s the matter, Larry?” asks Mule.

“Don’t worry, kid, we’ll have a good time in Boston too,” says Billy.

“It ain’t that. It’s me!”

“Whaddaya mean?”

“I’m a shitbird.”

“No you ain’t,” says Mule.

“You’re a good kid.”

“I’m a shitbird.”

“Why?”

“Oh, crap, I did a shitty thing.”

“What the hell did you do?”

Larry pulls up his jumper and stuck in his pants is Charlotte’s shepherd pipe. “I stole her goddamn pipe!”

Billy and Mule look at each other, cover their eyes and laugh, wailing and bouncing up and down.

“It’s not so fucking funny,” says Larry. “After she was so nice to me.”

“Christ, you really are a klepto, ain’t you?” says Billy.

"Well, it's not so funny! I don't care how big you are and if you are a first class."

"I'm sorry, Larry, I can't help what strikes me funny sometimes," says Billy.

"Me either," says Mule and bursts out laughing again, then forces himself to be sober.

When they are composed at last and Larry has taken the shepherd's pipe out of his pants, he asks, "Would you say I was a little . . . a little . . . gauche?"

Billy says, "Just a bit around the edges," and he and Mule break up again, Mule pounding the arms of his seat with his fist, Billy knocking the back of his head against the recliner.

"Goddamnit!" shouts Larry and throws the pipe down on the seat.

"Look it really ain't such a big thing," says Billy. "If it'll make you feel better, I'll take it back with us and tell her I put it in my AWOL bag by mistake."

"Oh sure, she's bound to believe that."

"She will. She knows me. I'm always doing stupid things like that."

"Will you? Will you call her from Boston and tell her I didn't steal it?"

"Sure, kid."

"All I wanted, you know, was something to remember by. They wouldn't let me keep a damn shepherd's pipe in the brig anyway."

"Probably not."

"Just tell her I didn't steal it, okay?"

"Okay."

"I don't want her thinking I'm gauche."

"She won't. Relax."

Half an hour later Larry says to Billy, "Would you get mad if I told you something?"

"Depends on what you tell me."

"Well, the reason I stole the shepherd's pipe and all is that I think I fell in love with your wife."

"She ain't my wife, Larry, she's up for grabs. You got as good a chance as the next dude."

"Ha, ha, ha. Hotel Alpha."

"No, I mean it."

"The thing is, I was thinking about making love to her. You know, screwing."

"You ever been laid?" Billy asks.

Larry fiddles with his fingers. "No."

"What the hell you been doing all these years?" says Mule.

"I don't know."

"Would you like to?" asks Billy.

"What?"

"Get laid."

"Sure, who wouldn't?"

"He's got you there," says Mule. "You can't keep aheada this kid."

"Would you mind making love to a whore?"

"You mean a prostitute-type whore?"

"Well, yeah, that's the kind I had in mind."

"Gee, I guess so, I'm not prejudiced."

"You're all right, kid," says Mule. "Not much to look at, but you're all right."

Six

In the Boston station Larry grabs Billy's arm and pulls him toward a phone booth to make the call to Charlotte. Billy says, "I'll call her if I can make up my own story, in my own way—alone." He shuts the door to the booth. Larry knocks on it and Billy opens it up.

"What now?"

"Do you have enough change?"

"Why? You gonna give me some?"

"No, I was only wondering . . ."

"Well, quit wondering 'cause I'm gonna reverse the charges."

"Maybe she'll be pissed and won't accept them."

"Will you cool it? You're beginning to sound like a goddamn Polish grandmother. Go fry some pierogies."

"But what if she doesn't?"

"Why the hell don't you just shut the hell up and see if she doesn't?"

He pulls the folding door and turns away.

"Okay, Billy," Larry mumbles.

Billy pushes his back against the door and pretends to be calling Charlotte. He does not want to talk to her so soon, even about something as detached as a shepherd's pipe. He does not want to talk to her until the detail is over and he knows what he wants to do. Once he knows, then there will be no trouble in the saying of it. He gabbles into the phone and occasionally raises his voice to say, "Is that right?" and "I'll be damned," or "Yeah, he's fine too." He looks over his shoulder to see if Larry is buying it. He smiles, nods his head, and points to the mouthpiece, in several short jabs. Billy puts the phone back on its hook and leaves the booth.

"What's the verdict?" asks Larry.

"Legal possession of a shepherd's pipe," says Billy.

"Huh?"

"I told her I packed the pipe by mistake and she said she wanted to give it to you anyway since you seemed to get a boot out of it, and when she noticed it was gone she figured she gave it to you the night before and just didn't remember because of the pot and all. Anyhow, she says for you to take it with her blessing and knock yourself out."

"No shit?"

"Absolute constipation."

"C'mon."

"I give you my word of honor as a representative of the president of the United States. She says you should keep the shepherd's pipe as a going away gift from her. I swear it on my life."

"That's good enough for me," says Larry, smiling widely. "What do you think of that, Mule?"

"You're a real meatman. Must am she has the hots for you—if you want Billy's retreads."

"What a thing to say! Damn, you could piss a guy off," says Larry.

Mule looks first at Billy, who is noncommittal, and then at Larry.

"Me?"

"You shouldn't talk like that about retreads. Women aren't tires," says Larry. "And besides, she doesn't even have the hots for me."

"Looks like it, that shepherd's pipe for a present. She didn't give no shepherd's pipe to Billy or me."

Larry opens his peacoat, lifts his jumper and pulls the shepherd's pipe out of his waistband. He holds it at arm's length in admiration and gratitude and wonder.

"Gee, I wonder if they'll let me keep it in the brig. What do you think, Billy?"

"I don't know about that. We could stow it in your AWOL bag and see what happens."

"Aw, they'll take one look at it and take it away. There's gotta be some regulation against it. Bother the other guys or something."

"Maybe not."

"Yeah, they'll probably take it away. Christ, what if they do? What if one of the guards just keeps it for himself? Charlotte's pipe. Oh, Christ. And tomorrow's the day."

"You gotta stop worrying about everything before it happens," says Billy.

"Yeah, that's easy for you to say, but *I'm* the one going to the brig, and she gave it to me."

"So take it and be happy, for Chrissake."

"How can you be happy even if you have a shepherd's pipe from Charlotte when you know that tomorrow they'll probably take it away from you?"

"Well, it ain't tomorrow yet," says Billy crossly.

"But it will *be* tomorrow in only a day," says Larry.

"Then play the fucking pipe today!" yells Billy.

"I gotch your fucking pipe—dangling!" yells Larry.

Billy chases him across the station floor, trying to connect with a good kick to the rear. Mule is right behind Billy, saying, "Cut the crap, Billy, there are civilians watching."

They are still wearing their guns and SP bands.

Billy stops chasing the boy. Larry sticks his hands into his jacket pockets and waits for them at the far end of the platform.

"They're gonna court-martial me some one of these days," says Billy to Mule, "and it'll be for murder. I'm gonna kill that little bastard."

They check into a third-rater and stow their gear and hit the streets to kill the time until nightfall.

They see a small white block building of one story, or less, depending upon how stories are measured, off by itself next to a parking lot. On the outboard of this building is a little alcove for a shoeshine parlor, exposed on one side to the weather. On the building itself, in large red letters, is printed one word: TATTOOS.

They go inside. Behind a railing to the left are two sets of chairs facing each other. Captain Joe, identified by his name plate on the counter next to him, his arms a mass of dark blue figures, sits in one chair and has his feet on the empty one in front of him. His wife, Mrs. Captain Joe, is putting the finishing touches on a customer, a young Italian kid who has three friends leaning over the rail and watching the action, giving him the verbal needle as Mrs. Captain Joe give him the electric needle. She has done the head and bust of a girl from one of the many plastic templates of girls available, suitable for a young stud's bicep. One bare breast hangs over a flowing banner, on which will be written a girl's name, but not tonight. The Italian kid wants to give more thought to that.

"Quit squirming," laughs one of the spectators.

"It don't hurt," says the client. "Where are your balls?"

"I'm no goddamn Indian. My old lady'd chase me outa the house with a broom if I came home with a naked girl on my arm," says the spectator.

"It's my goddamn arm, ain't it?"

Billy and Mule and Larry look at the samples behind glass covers that fill up the wall space in the parlor.

"Here's a nice black panther," says Billy. "Just right for a militant like you."

"Yeah, it'd almost show up too, wouldn't it? Here's the one for you. Donald Duck in a sailor cap smoking a corncob pipe. And look what it says below it—'*So What.*'"

They point out to each other the ones that strike their fancies: big red crab with the words *Bite Me* below it; a drunken marine, below him *U.S.M.C.,* above him, *Never Again;* a shattered heart, a banner across the heart with capital letters, DECIEVED.

"I'm not gonna have this dude write anything on my bod," says Billy. "The poor simp can't even spell."

"Looks all right to me," says Mule.

"*I* before *e* except after *c,* shitferbrains."

"I'm glad I teamed up with a smart bastard like you. You must be one of them sexual intellectuals I been hearing about."

"Huh?" says Larry.

"A fucking know-it-all."

"Yuk, yuk," says Billy and hand-signals, YANKEE UNIFORM, KILO, YANKEE, UNIFORM, KILO.

"Got a seat free, navy," says Captain Joe. "Sailor ain't a sailor till a sailor's been tattooed. That's in a famous song. How about an anchor with *Underway Again*?"

"What about it, Larry? Want a tattoo?" asks Billy.

"No, I don't think so," says Larry, feeling uncomfortable here somehow.

"What about a flag with *Duty First*?" asks Captain Joe.

"Negative," says Mule.

"Do you have anything with a religious theme? My friend here is a very religious-type fella," says Billy, indicating Mule.

"Are you kidding? This is religious tattoo headquarters. Approved by the Pope and Billy Graham theirselves. I got a red cross with lilies that's a beauty. Write anything you want above it."

"Thing is," says Billy, "my friend here just became a Buddhist. Got any Buddhist tattoos?"

"Look, don't waste my time if you don't want nothing."

"I'm serious. Lay a little chant on him, Mule."

"Ain't got no damn Buddhist tattoo," says Captain Joe. "What about a skull and *Death Before Dishonor*?"

"Nope," says Mule.

"*Born to Raise Hell*?"

"Nope."

"Ain't got no damn Buddhist tattoo. Everything I got is on the bulkheads."

Mrs. Captain Joe has finished her job. She washes the new tattoo and tells him whatever he does to let the scab drop off by itself. She puts a paper napkin over the tattoo and fastens it to his arm with Scotch tape.

On the wall behind her is an eight and a half by eleven picture of a young man. Except for a nasty scowl, his face looks normal enough. His entire torso, however, is a nightmare of pythons, panthers, daggers, skulls, vultures—a regular Vincent Price double feature. Printed above the picture are the words, "Tattooed by Biggs & Squire, Chatham Sq., N.Y."

"No wonder he looks so pissed off," says Billy. "What a way to break into the advertising business."

The door opens and a nattily dressed black man enters, followed by the round-shouldered, droopy-lipped shoeshine boy from the adjacent alcove.

Captain Joe's deep rumble fills the room. "Get the hell outa here! I told you before, dammit, I don't want you coming in here hustlin' shines."

The shoeshine boy looks at him with hurt in his eyes. "I wasn't even hustlin' shines."

"I don't give a shit what you were doing! Get your ass outa here or I'll drop a bowling ball on your punkin head."

"That'll be the day," says the shoeshine boy.

"We'll putcha outa business, you bastard, if you don't keep outa here. You won't *have* a shoeshine business," adds Mrs. Captain Joe.

"That'll be the day," he says, shutting the door behind him.

"Well," says Mule to Billy, "do you want a tattoo?"

"Does a nun want the clap? I got my tattoos already—on the inside—and they ain't red crosses and lilies."

"Maybe we should get the first-class chevrons tattooed on our arms. I got a feeling they ain't going to be on our sleeve for long," says Mule.

On the street again, Larry amuses himself by window shopping at the pawnshops. Billy and Mule stay one storefront behind him.

"What did you mean by that last crack?" asks Billy.

"Well, you're planning on taking him to a whorehouse, ain't you?"

"Not if you don't want to."

"Do *you* want to?"

"Doesn't make a rat's ass to me. A chevron's just a chevron when you come down to it."

"I was only thinking that with our luck the goddamn place would be busted and there we are, two chasers and a prisoner. Outstanding."

"The thing is, the kid's eighteen and he never had it. Next chance he gets he'll be twenty-six, and God knows what'll happen by that time. By that time he might not even want it any more, you know what I mean? It'd be good to remember what it's like."

"Yeah, but—"

"You either want to or you don't want to, one. Which?"

"Eighteen. I got laid first time when I was about eleven or twelve. The girl was eighteen, for Chrissake. And, hell, I was a deprived black kid from the South."

"I was fourteen. In the icehouse. Remember I told you about the icehouse?"

"That must've been a frosty first."

"Brrr."

"Look at that damn kid," says Mule. "He sure ain't had much out of it."

"His life, you mean?"

"He sure ain't had much fun."

"He's a good kid, though," says Billy. "He's got a heart in the right place."

"But not a bunch of fun."

"Well?"

"Hell, it don't make a rat's ass to me neither. I never been in a house that was busted yet. If he wants to go, well, hell, let's take him, eighteen years old."

They catch up with Larry and Billy says, "Remember earlier on the train I asked you about getting laid?"

"Sure."

"Well, what about it?"

"Whaddaya mean, what about it?"

"Do you want to?"

"You mean here in Boston?"

"Well, you just think about that for a minute."

Larry thinks, then smiles at his own forgetfulness.

"You know where there's a place?"

"There are ways," says Billy.

"Wow, you mean like right now, huh? Just go ahead and do it?"

"Not this exact instant, but later on this evening."

"You know, I think I would. Just like that. Get the old ashes hauled."

Billy and Mule look at each other. "*Ashes hauled*?"

"That's an expression, kinda like, that means, you know, to do it, get it done."

"Jesus, the kid's from another planet," says Billy.

"The thing is," says Larry, "what about the money?"

"I wish you'd drop that subject too. The *last* thing in the world to worry about, if you're the kinda fart that has to worry about something, is money. What's a friend for if he can't buy a friend a piece of tail when he needs it?"

"I'm sure game if you and Mule are," says Larry.

They catch a movie to kill a few hours because according to Billy, "It's good to get there early before the juice is outa them but not so early that they're still half asleep yet."

Larry sits between Mule and Billy and during the movie bugs each of them in turn:

"We don't even know where the place is."

"We'll find it."

"How much will it cost, do you think?"

"Don't sweat it. It's our treat."

"Well, what do I say to her?"

"Let nature take its course."

"Do they assign you one or do you hafta make up your own mind?"

"You make up your mind. The US Navy ain't running whore-houses yet."

"I don't know what to do. Do I just go ahead and start undressing or what?"

"You let her take care of everything. She knows what to do. This won't be her first time."

"How many times do you figure she did it? You know, altogether?"

"Will you shut the fuck up? I want to see what this dude's going to do now that they knocked off his kid brother."

"I didn't mean any offense. I just wanna know, so I don't come off like some kinda dumbbell."

"Relax, for Chrissake. They're used to dumbbells."

"Maybe so, but I don't wanna come off like one anyway."

They leave the movie, unable to pass even the most elementary critical judgment on it. They stop a seaman on the street and Billy says, "Tell me there, partner, you wouldn't know where a man could get laid around here for money, would you?"

"I always try the nurses' home," says the seaman.

"Make out pretty well there, do you?"

"I ain't hurtin'," says the seaman.

"Well, the thing is, partner, we don't have the time for howdy-do, dance-around-the-parlor first," says Billy.

"Try the nurses' home, it don't take so long." The seaman walks away.

"Hell," says Larry, "we aren't even gonna get to first base, I bet."

"O ye of little faith. I wanna know who you're talking to. Is this the original Bad-Ass or is this some candy-ass seaman playing Scrabble at the goddamn nurses' home?"

"It's the original Bad-Ass," says Larry devoutly.

"You better bereave it," says Billy.

They stand on the curb at an intersection and check out the cabs as they drive by.

"What are we doing?" asks Larry.

"Cabbies know where to get laid, only they don't always tell you."

"What about this one off the port side?" asks Mule.

"Huh-uh. Four eyes. People with glasses give me a peculiar feeling. 'Specially cab drivers."

They allow several others to pass by until finally Billy spots *the* cab driver. "He's over forty, got a silly wool hat and a suede jacket. He's the one."

Mule and Larry get in the back, Billy sits next to the driver.

"Hyuh, partner, how they treating you?" says Billy.

"Fine. Where to?"

"Just down the street here. Well, hell. I'll tell you exactly what we want. You look honest. I trust you."

Billy pauses but the cabbie will not fill the hole.

"We're in transit, the three of us, and we could sure use the services of a decent cathouse that don't hate G.I.'s."

The cabbie says nothing.

"Sizeable tip in it for you."

Still nothing.

"C'mon, mister, give us a break. I wouldn't press if it wasn't important."

"Relax. It ain't far. And save your tip. I get a tip on the other end," says the cabbie. "I been in transit a few times myself. I'm an old minesweep sailor."

"Well, hellfire, I'm happy to be in your company. The minesweep guys are a real ballsy bunch."

There is not enough time for a full-length sea story, so they listen instead to fragments of memories told with equal portions of pride, joy, and sorrow. The cabbie says, "I guess you can take a man outa the navy but you can't take the navy outa the man."

"That's a definite fact, well said," says Billy. "What do you think, Mule?"

"A definite fact. Right, Larry?"

"I guess so," says Larry.

As the cabbie pulls into the driveway between clumps of trees that encircle and practically hide the small white house, he says, "Now getta load of this."

They drive over a service station bell hose and hear from inside the single "ding" of the bell. An older woman, obviously the boss lady, looks out of a window. She greets them at the door. "Hi, Lou, how's the boy?"

"Right as rain, Millie. Got a few live ones for you."

"C'mon in, boys, navy's always welcome here. Welcome aboard, as they say."

They enter into a brightly lit room, too brightly lit, with a well-waxed linoleum floor and an abundance of deck furniture on which have been sitting seven girls in short shorts and halters, who now jump up and form a line facing the sailors.

"As the blind man said when he passed the fish market, hello girls," says Mule.

There is no response from the girls. The temperature of the room is eighty degrees. They hear the "ding" of the departing cab.

Billy unbuttons his peacoat and says, "Gee, Millie, what you should do here is cover the floor with sand and you'd have one hell of a beach."

Millie laughs and says, "That's a damn good idea. I'm gonna hafta think about that one."

"Got a friend here we wanta do a favor for. Going away on a trip."

"Are you two going to get pussy or just the kid?"

"Just the kid, Millie," says Mule.

"What kind of party do you want?"

"Well, it's the kid's party," says Billy. "He'll call it."

"Pick a winner," says Billy.

Larry goes down the line of girls and back again. His manner is self-conscious and tentative. This is the original dirty dream in three dimensions. He gives the nod to the one who looks the youngest, a short, attractive whore with light brown hair. As they walk to an adjoining bedroom, Billy intercepts her and presses an extra five dollar bill into her hand without Millie seeing.

"Make it a good one, baby, it has to last a *long* time," he tells her.

She steals a glance at the bill and holds her hand tightly around it. "Sure, honey, anything you say," she says and with her other hand gives Billy a sharp pinch to the thigh.

Billy joins Mule on two side-by-side chaise lounges and says, "Damned if I wouldn'ta picked the same whore. She's a cute little thing. Whaddaya think?"

"No matter to me," says Mule. "They're all the wrong color."

"Oh, come off that shit," says Billy. "I've had them in all colors. Don't make any difference."

"Maybe to you it don't," says Mule and sits with his arms folded across his chest. "But *I* got racial pride."

"Are you giving me a ration?" says Billy.

Mule explodes into laughter and says, "Yeah!" and thumps Billy on the arm.

After a moment, Billy says, "Seriously, though, do you go more for one or more for the other?"

"I'll admit," says Mule, "I used to like white chicks best, but now the member chicks are changing. Used to be that a member chick was interested in one thing—cash. If you didn't have bread she wasn't gonna begin to drop pants for you because she didn't wanta wind up like her momma, know what I mean? So a member chick would hafta know you had money before she would let herself go even a little bit. And if she was really something else, you know, a Barbara McNair or a Diahann Carroll or something like that, then she only played around with honkies. That's the way it used to be, man."

"Didn't it piss you off?"

"No, man, I understood. I figured if I was a chick I'd do the same way. But that's changin' now and it's all on accounta one person and I ain't shittin'—Stokely Carmichael. That cat done more for bringing black men and chicks together than any friggin organization ever did. Because he convinced us, man, that we were *beautiful*, and we never believed it before. I heard him say once on TV, he said, 'We are *black*, we have *kinky hair*, we have *broad noses*, we have *full lips*, and we are *beautiful*, man!' You don't know what it is to have a cat rattle off the things that make you different whack, whack, whack! Then tell you, man, you're *so* lucky to be that way. If I ever have a kid or a dog or anything, I'm gonna name him Stokely. That's one beautiful nigger."

"Hey, man, that kinda talk is un-American," says Billy. "I read once on one of my paperback covers that the American Legion gave us when I was a kid that to call some dude a nigger is definitely un-American. Yes sir."

"It ain't un-American for *me*. Know what I'd like to hear sometime?"

"What?"

"I'd like to hear somebody say that some kinda talk is un-Canadian or un-Spanish or un-Yugoslavian or something."

"Why, you dumb clown, you wouldn't know if you heard it. What the hell do you know in Yugoslavian?"

"Well, I know there ain't no such thing as un-Yugoslavian."

"I guess we'd have to talk to a Yugoslavian about that, wouldn't we?" says Billy. "Hey, any of you ladies Yugoslavian?"

A few girls look up from their magazines and fingernails.

"We're all American girls here," says one. "I'm from Akron."

"Would you settle for half-Austrian?" asks another.

"How about a nice Roman Catholic?" says the third.

Billy turns back to Mule. "Should I ask her if anything can be un-half-Austrian?"

"I gotch your un-half-Austrian swinging."

"Hey sweetheart," Billy says to the half Austrian.

"You know about being un-American? You know, like to call a guy nigger or Polack is un-American. Do you know, since you're half-Austrian, if anything can be *un*-half-Austrian?"

"Feel your head, sailor, you're sick."

"Just trying to be friendly," says Billy.

"I can't eat tomorrow on friendly. Let's go to a room."

"See, Mule," says Billy, "that's what it's all come to. My book covers were full of shit. Everyone wants to go to a room instead of being American."

"Cheapskate," says the whore.

"If you're a good girl I'll give you a great big kiss for free when we leave."

"And a case of trenchmouth, I bet. I may look like a whale, babes, but I'm no fish. Keep your kisses for your girlfriend and give me cash. I'm saving my mouth for the man I marry."

He signals with his hands: HOTEL ALPHA, HOTEL ALPHA. She returns to her magazine. He is bored with her too.

He lies back in the chaise and shuts his eyes and sees all the whorehouses, all the bar hookers he's had—the five and the two's: five for the girl and two for the room. He never met the stereotype whore with the heart of gold, but most of them were pretty nice kids who knew what they wanted—and probably knew the chances were against their ever getting it: the apartment house, an education, a little beer bar. Just a couple more years, they figured, and they would get out while the getting was good. Billy wonders if he doesn't have the same pipe dream, for he sometimes must think of himself as a whore. *What is it that he's saving for?* he wonders, and he wonders if along with the cash the whores haven't taken that which cannot be made again.

He can't remember names anymore, just places: Pottsville, Brooklyn, Port Clinton, Chicago, San Diego, Norfolk, Palma, Barcelona, Naples, Valetta, Tokyo, San Juan, C. Z., on and on and on. The places connect in his mind as neatly as links on a chain. Only in Palma when he was just a seaman did a girl kiss him during the paid performance of love. It was a slight brush of the lips to show she liked him. Before he went back to the ship he gave her all the money he had. He can't remember now how much it was, but it was all the money he had.

Larry finally comes out and it's clear he's had their money's worth. He looks like a small boy following a grin.

The whore comes out after him and says, "He's quite a man."

Billy and Mule each put a hand on a shoulder and give him a paternal shake. They are glad that this at least has gone well for them. They are three sailors on good liberty.

Confidentially the whore whispers to Billy before they leave, "I been with sailors before, lotsa them, but I never seen one bring a damn piccolo to a cathouse before. Is he all right?"

Seven

LARRY, OF COURSE, CAN SPEAK of nothing else. Upon awaking in the morning he begins the conversation not where it left off last night after cheeseburgers, fries, and a new level of beer, but in the middle somewhere. Billy and Mule were sick of hearing it last night, but this morning they welcome his reliving the experience. This is the last day.

Larry stands at the bathroom door and talks to Billy as he shaves. Mule is putting his things in his bag.

"The door wasn't even completely shut, you know, before she turned around and started undoing the buttons to my pants. Before I knew it, the flap falls open in front and she's digging around in there."

"What's she say again?"

"'Let me check out your peter, honey.' I swear to God! Like I'm a car in a gas station and she's checking the oil. My knees were shaking a mile a minute but I just stood there and figured she knew what she was doing."

"I told you she would."

"I was so scared I was afraid it wouldn't come up. I'd never live that down."

"Did it come up all right?"

"Did it! Boy, I couldn't even bend my fingers or blink my eyes! I didn't have the skin left."

Billy and Mule laugh at the old joke.

"Well, welcome to the wonderful world of pussy," says Billy.

"You know, it was all cut and dried and I guess I'm supposed to feel guilty. But, I don't. I really don't. It's probably sinful, but I *liked* it!"

"I kinda figured maybe you did," says Mule.

"I had the feeling she liked me too. She was really with it, you know, in bed. Okay, maybe it was just an act for her, but for me it was real and that's what counts."

"They got feelings like anyone else. She probably did like you," says Billy.

"Even so, it's not the same, I guess, as doing it with someone you love. Huh, Mule?"

Mule stops what he is doing and looks at Larry for a moment, but does not answer.

"Huh, Billy?" asks Larry.

Billy rinses out his razor and drops it into his douche kit. "Okay, kid," he says "the sink is yours."

Larry opens his own douche kit and says, "Like you said, I guess I got a knack for bringing things to a close."

He lathers his face and begins to shave.

They check out of the hotel, wearing arms, and have coffee in a place next door. The silence is uncalm, and the way Billy leans back against the wall and stretches a leg across the seat of the booth, the way Mule puts one leg over his knee and then in a minute changes it, the way Larry leans his forehead over his coffee against his propped up hand, reveal them going down inside.

Since Larry is the cause of their depression, he feels obliged to say something.

"It's nice to sit here and drink coffee and not be a cherry any more," says Larry.

The other two do not take it up. Larry blows on his coffee, then says, "Okay, when do we go?"

"Where?" says Billy, not looking at him.

"Ha, ha."

"The orders say prior to twenty-four hundred," says Billy.

"So when do we go?"

"Whenever you feel like it prior to twenty-four hundred. Mule?"

"Right," says Mule, giving a thumbs-up signal.

"It's been a very nice trip and now it's over," says Larry. "Thanks."

"You don't hafta get there until twenty-four hundred," says Billy.

"There ain't nothing left to do."

"We could go see a movie or two," says Mule.

"Maybe get a couple of six-packs," says Billy.

"Shitfire, if you wanta, we can even go back to the cathouse," says Mule.

"No, I don't think so. If it's only the one time, that makes that one time stick out, know what I mean?"

"Yeah," says Billy.

"Anyhow, I don't like to go to a new station after dark. Makes me feel lonelier than hell. Silly I guess."

"Well, we got a bunch of hours before dark and the bus to Portsmouth is only about an hour'n a half," says Billy.

"Looks like it's gonna be a nice day too," says Mule.

"If it was summer, we could maybe have a picnic," says Larry. "That'd be nice."

They go back to their coffee and are silent again for a few minutes.

"There's nothin' saying we can't," says Billy at last. "We could anyway."

"Could what?" says Mule.

"Why, have a goddamn picnic!"

They go to a vest-pocket wilderness south of Hyde Park and struggle with a slippery incline, carrying hot dogs, onions, mustard, pretzels, and beer in large brown grocery bags. On top of the grocery bags they have put their AWOL bags.

"Jesus Christ, there's snow all over the ground," says Mule.

"Of course there's snow all over the ground," answers Billy. "So what?"

"So, I'm just sayin' there is."

"C'mon, guys," says Larry.

"And if I'm permitted to state one more fact," says Mule, "my goddamn gonies are frozen."

"Many are cold but few are frozen," says Billy.

"Whatever the hell that's supposed to mean," says Mule.

"There's a fireplace thing up there on the level," says Larry. "We can build a fire and warm up."

"I'm for that," says Mule. "I'm a Lousyana boy."

They gather dry firewood from under the surrounding evergreens and break the thin sticks over their knees, each time careful to brush off their wool pants. The thicker sticks they lean against the fireplace and jump on them, breaking them into good sizes. They enjoy it and take turns jumping and cracking the sticks.

They get kindling and spread it at the base of the fireplace. Carefully they stack the smaller sticks on top of the kindling. Billy lights it with cupped hands and blows on the flame almost lovingly until the smaller sticks ignite. They add thicker sticks and soon the fire is high and strong and hot.

They turn their backsides to it and crowd together, shuffling about to avoid the smoke. They feel the heat of the fire sear through their uniforms and soon it is too hot for Billy and Larry. Mule stays a few minutes longer until it is too hot even for a Lousyana boy.

They pull the tabs from three cans and drink beer and munch on pretzels. During the second round of beers they begin to feel cold again and move closer to the fire. They face it this time, shoulders touching, and tilt their beer cans to their mouths.

"Well, here we are," says Billy, "having an All-American backyard barbecue, just like the decent people."

"Yep," says Larry, "just like we knew what we were doing."

"What the hell *do* you do on a cook-out, picnic-type of thing?" asks Mule.

"You never been on a *picnic*?" asks Billy.

"Nope."

"Me neither," says Larry.

Billy thinks for a moment and throws his empty beer can into the fire. It sputters for a few seconds.

"Christ All Friday," he says. "Some All-Americans. I never have neither."

"Well, there's no law says everybody has to be on a picnic before a special age," says Larry.

"No, but it would be nice to know what the hell you're doing," says Billy.

"What's to do?" says Larry. "You just go out and cook hot dogs on the fire and have fun. Everybody knows that. It's no big deal you have to learn."

"Pretty lucky for us."

They clear a place in front of the fire and cover it with evergreen branches. They sit down on the branches and put hot dogs on the ends of sticks to hold them over the fire. They hold them directly over the flame and in short order they are black, but the sailors do not mind. They have forgotten to buy buns so they take turns dipping their hot dogs, still attached to the sticks, into the mustard jar, and alternating between bites of hot dog they eat the onions like apples. Larry, who doesn't like onions that much, breathes heavily after each bite.

"Dear Mom," says Billy, "you'll be happy to know we had a wonderful Christmas dinner. Tube steak a la fire with an array of condiments."

After their meal they light up cigarettes and open beers and lean back on their elbows, watching the flames. They give themselves up to it for a few moments.

"This ain't bad," says Mule.

"It's better than a kick in the head with a icy galosh," says Billy.

"It's better than lots of things," adds Larry, and they go back to their private thoughts.

Billy watches the fire crack and jump, conscious of being next to two friends, more than friends because they are going *through* something together. The fire is warm, the air is cold and fresh and clean, the day is sunny. And he asks himself why, in the midst of this goodness, why does he see in his mind the Cairo Club in Long Beach, California.

Why does he see himself swaggering, biting down a cigarette in the style made famous by James Dean, showing his I. D. to the bouncer at the door, having a pasty-faced bar girl stamp on his hand three red letters: CAI, for Cairo Club. He pays fifty cents to get inside and he pays seventy-five cents for a bottle of beer and there is nothing there but sailors and women who are not too ugly or too old, who will sit with the sailors at tables and allow them to buy champagne cocktails and will smile and try to get their cigarette lighters, their rings, their cash.

He can hear the jukebox, at shattering volume, playing hillbilly songs that were popular five years before. He can see himself push open the red plastic-padded door with the studs driven into it to spell *MEN*. The walls are damp, the floor is wet, the unshaded bulb is glaring. Two exposed toilets face two urinals. They are a foot apart and the single roll of toilet paper sits on the wet floor between them.

He can see himself taking a leak and looking at a vending machine next to him. Your choice for a quarter: a heads-tails key chain, a "gag gift," a pixie deck of cards (complete deck), a packet of four buttons: *Happiness is a warm pussy. If it feels good do it. Sex has no calories. Use contraceptives—no deposit, no return.*

He asks himself why, in the midst of this goodness, why does he see the whores instead of Charlotte. *You leave more with a whore than an ounce of salt water and a bit of cash,* he thinks. *What does she leave with you?*

"Here we are," he says out loud, "three pals on a picnic. Do we think about other picnics? No, we ain't even been on one before. We never ice skated, we never seen the sights, all we know is whores and bars."

"We know ships," says Mule, "and we know our rate."

"Yeah, whores and bars and ships and our rates."

"That counts for something," says Mule.

"What?"

"Well, I know it's gotta count for something, service to your country."

Larry has not been listening. During their exchange he was humming softly, and now he sings, "*Eternal Father, strong to save, whose arm hath bound the restless wave . . .*" Billy and Mule join in "*. . . Who bidd'st the mighty ocean deep, its own appointed limits keep, O hear us when we cry to Thee for those in peril on the sea.*"

"The Navy Hymn," says Larry. "I learned it by heart."

"Yeah," says Mule.

"If only that's what it was all about," says Billy, too vague to be questioned.

"I don't guess it'll get any better than it is right now," says Larry. "Might as well go and get it over with."

"We still got a bunch of hours till nightfall," says Billy.

"Pretty puny bunch," says Larry.

"There's still a couple of things we can do," says Billy.

"Like what?" says Mule.

"Well, like for instance, supposing I pick up my bad old ass and supposing I bend down and get me a good scoop of snow like this here and supposing I pack it real hard like this here and supposing . . ."

Mule is on his feet and running in one direction. Larry in the other. Billy throws the snowball and nicks Mule on the shoulder. Mule makes a snowball and returns the fire, just missing Billy's ear. Billy is laughing and bends down to make another snowball when he notices that Larry is still running.

"Son-of-a-bitch! He's running away!" yells Billy. Everything happens with incredible speed. Larry is running across an open field of snow, lifting his knees high as he runs. Billy draws the .45 and runs several steps forward. He has the ammo clip in his left hand and is about to ram it into the .45.

"Jesus Christ, Billy!" yells Mule.

Billy stops and looks at his hands, a gun in one, an ammo clip in the other. "My God!" He throws them down into the snow and starts running after Larry. He runs fast but Larry has a good head start and Billy knows he will tire first.

As he runs a losing race, Billy surprises himself by chanting. "*Nam-Myoho-Renge-Kyo, Nam-Myoho-Renge-Kyo, Nam-Myoho-Renge-Kyo . . . stop,* you son-of-a-bitch . . . *Nam-Myoho-Renge-Kyo* . . . at least slow down, you bastard . . . *Nam-Myoho-Renge-Kyo.*"

Larry falls down in the snow, skidding on his shoulder. He lies face up on the ground and rubs his shoulder, making no attempt to get up and run again.

When Billy reaches him, he throws himself on top of Larry, straddling his midsection and holding down his wrists.

"Goddamn you! What kind of sailor are you, you son-of-a-bitch. All personnel in the Naval Service must show in themselves a good example of subordination, courage, zeal, sobriety, neatness, and attention to *duty*! *Duty!*"

It trips out of his mouth word by word.

Mules catches up to them. He has Billy's gun and ammo clip in his hands.

"You ain't no good sailor!" yells Billy, only inches away from Larry's face.

"You ain't neither!" yells Larry.

Billy slaps him twice across the face, once with his palm and again with the back of his hand.

"Give me a ship, you little prick! Give me a ship!"

"I'm sorry, Billy," says Larry.

Billy rolls off him and lies next to him in the snow, panting.

"I wasn't really running away," says Larry.

"Yeah?" says Mule, who sits down in the snow next to Larry.

"Huh-uh. I was just running is all."

"But, not away," says Mule.

"Nope. Just running."

Billy's breathing becomes more regular but he says nothing.

"Anyway, you didn't shoot me," says Larry.

"Son-of-a-bitch," says Billy

"I said I was sorry."

"Son-of-a-bitch anyway," says Billy.

"You're the best damn sailor I ever knew," says Larry. "You and Mule both."

"Goddamnit, you're going to the brig today," says Billy. "That's what the orders say and that's as sure as this snow on the ground."

"Well, hell, I know that," says Larry.

"Damn well better," says Billy.

"This don't make much good sense to me," says Mule.

Billy pulls himself up and helps Larry to a sitting position. Once again Larry says, "I'm sorry."

"I'm sorry too, kid. I didn't have to slap you around like that."

"Doesn't matter. It was my own fault. I have a stupid mouth. Stupid mouth and sticky fingers. I need a vet. I got a rare hoof-and-mouth disease."

They laugh, slowly and quietly, hoping to laugh away the tension, and as they laugh, Larry is pushing away the layer of snow in front of his knees. He uncovers grass, wet and green, waiting for spring. Instinctively, he pulls a bit of it up, sticks it into his mouth and chews it. Billy and Mule, simultaneously, follow suit and stick wads of grass into their mouths. Soon they are laughing loudly at each other, chomping down on mouthfuls of wet grass like three stray head of cattle.

Suddenly Larry stops laughing and says, "Oh-oh, I just thought of something I haven't thought about since I was a little kid."

"What's that?"

"I just thought, what if plants and weeds and grass 'n stuff can *feel* it when they're pulled out of the ground and killed? They're living things, you know. When I was a kid, pulling weeds, I thought maybe someday they'd get even with me."

"Where'd you get a screwball notion like that?" asks Mule.

"Wait a minute," says Billy. "How the hell do you know? How can *anyone* know, man? Getting killed *hurts.* It hurts if you're a man or a dog or a bug. So it may hurt if you're nothing but a blade of grass."

They spit into their hands, look at the mashed grass, and wipe their hands with snow.

"I ain't gonna do that anymore," says Larry.

"Me neither," says Billy.

"Me neither," says Mule.

"Looks like a coupla old dogs learning some new tricks," says Billy.

Larry rises and gives a hand to each of the other two and helps them to their feet.

"Is it okay then?" asks Larry. "About the misunderstanding?"

"Sure," says Billy. "I learned a new trick."

"Besides," says Mule, "the exercise was good for us. Billy ain't run so far so fast since the fleet come in early and he was in the wrong bedroom."

They walk slowly back to their fire and stand in front of it. Soon vapor rises from their wet wool uniforms. They drink another round of beers. Wordless, they take a long look around them, at the evergreen trees, at the snowy fields, at the sky above.

Evergreen trees become chain-link fencing. Snowy fields become concrete grinders where men are mustered, marched, and sometimes manhandled. The days they've spent together are gone. The actual trip has vanished, and it is by some oddity of time and nature that they walk across the brig compound, the late winter sun casting shadows of the wire squares of the fence on the concrete deck, across which passes also the shadow of a gull.

They are led now by a marine guard. The chasers keep their faces front, watching the khaki figure ahead of them, the suggestion of short bristles of hair just below the cap, but Larry swivels his head, taking in the grimness of the military prison like a deep breath of carbon monoxide. Three sets of shoulders seem weighed down by the ugliness of this place. Larry cannot believe that Mule and Billy will go away and leave him here. This is not the place for it. He hopes that at least they will stay with him. This is no place to be alone.

With both hands he clutches Billy's arm, puts his face against the wool of Billy's sleeve, and even as they continue walking, he cries like a young widow.

"Steady kid," says Billy. "Steady. We're gonna check in with the OOD is all. It'll be okay."

Billy's voice cracks. He puts his hand on the back of Larry's head. He has dislocated the position of Larry's white hat. He straightens it for him.

The marine looks over his shoulder with half a smile on his face, his eyes like green reflectors, his arms swinging mechanically by his side.

"You want something, Pfc?" says Mule.

"Nope," says the marine and turns around.

"Good," says Mule. It is feeble, he knows, and he would like to say more, but he knows he must shut up for Larry's sake.

Larry straightens himself out by the time they are led into the office of the Officer of the Day, a marine who sits behind his desk and is now sipping coffee from a white mug that has painted on it the narrow silver bar that represents his rank, first lieutenant.

Sailors do not salute in offices. Instead the three come to attention in a line before his desk and Billy gives him their orders.

"First Class Petty Officers Buddusky and Mulhall, sir, reporting as ordered with Seaman Meadows, a prisoner."

"Seaman recruit, looks like. At ease," says the OOD. "How long does the prisoner have to serve?"

"Eight years," says Billy.

The OOD takes another sip of coffee. "Don't look so glum. It's really only six."

They are pleased and bewildered and look at each other.

"Two are knocked off at the beginning for good behavior. 'Course, if you fuck up . . ."

Larry immediately thinks in terms of six years now, but Mule and Billy look at the grunt standing to the side at parade rest and know that it's a rare fish that can live for six years in these waters with these sharks and not be chewed up.

The OOD looks at Larry's records and their orders. He turns up the corners of his mouth in disgust and tosses the bundle back on his desk. He takes another sip of coffee, and replaces the cup carefully on a felt pad.

"You haven't left yet," he says.

"Sir?"

"Your orders weren't endorsed when you left, so according to this, you're still in Norfolk."

This is the officer's way of saying that orders must be endorsed at departure and arrival, but this is something that both Billy and Mule know very well already, as well as they know that occasionally a mistake is made and orders are not endorsed at one point or another and it doesn't mean a damn thing.

"Well, we're standing here in front of you sir," says Billy.

The OOD smiles. "Yes, but you haven't left yet."

It reminds Billy of the kind of game his father liked to play, the object of which was to prove that he was smarter than his son.

"If we haven't left yet," says Billy, "then we don't have a prisoner with us. We're still getting drunk in Norfolk. We'll just go out and let this man go free."

Larry's face brightens and Billy is sorry he has spoken. Larry believes that Billy has won the game of logic and now can actually let him go free. He thinks the navy must have some provision for outsmarting marine officers.

"Don't give me any of your damn insolence, sailor!" shouts the OOD, slamming his desk with his hand. "You're addressing a first lieutenant in the Corps."

Mule finally speaks up. "We respectfully request to see the executive officer, *sir*."

"Another country heard from," says the OOD. "Who do you think *you* are?"

"A first class petty officer with time in. Between the two of us we have damn near thirty years in this navy. That's a lotta time. Do you think we're gonna stand here and be hard-assed because some dude in Norfolk forgot to endorse our orders?"

"You're going to get in a parcel of trouble, boy, I don't care how much time in," says the OOD. "The navy is built on chain of command and strict discipline, boy. Discipline."

"I know what the navy is built on," says Mule. "It took me a pile of years to find out. It's built on bullshit and rednecks like you who like to call niggers boy."

The marine guard makes a movement toward them. Billy turns to him and says, "You stay right where you are, grunt."

The marine looks at the OOD.

"You guys are going to be in deep trouble, what I mean," says the OOD. "You're going to find yourself staying here with your buddy."

Larry looks from one man to another, confused and frightened. Mule and Billy stand steadfast.

"I am not going to say another word, *sir*. We'll tell it all to the XO," says Mule.

"And what makes you think the XO can be bothered with a little detail like this? I'll endorse your damn orders and you can get the hell out of here."

He looks at the clock and scribbles on their orders and slaps them on the forward edge of his desk.

"You're supposed to pull a few copies," says Billy.

Furious now, the OOD pulls his copies.

"Now, haul ass," he says, "and pray to God I never see you two brought in here. You'll never leave."

Larry knows for certain now that the trip is over. Once again he clutches Billy's sleeve and begins to whimper. "I'm scared," he whispers.

"We got to go, Larry," says Billy, holding him and patting him on the back a few times. "There's no selection. Be a good man. Do your time. Don't give anybody a ration of shit, and you'll make out all right. You'll see. If you need anything, write me at the transient barracks in Norfolk. They'll know where I've gone. So long, kid."

"So long, Larry," says Mule and shakes his shoulder.

"Take that crybaby to indoctrination and start making a man out of him," the OOD tells the marine. "The ladies will find their own way out," he adds in an effeminate voice.

In his mind, Billy sees himself drawing the .45 and taking careful aim with a straight arm. He squeezes back the trigger and his hand jerks up with the recoil. The single .45 slug enters the OOD's forehead, shattering it like safety glass. When it exits from the back of his head it takes with it huge clumps of hair, handfuls of bone and brain, and a steamer track of blood. The Pfc. falls upon him and tears at the corpse with his teeth.

Larry lets go of Billy's sleeve and tries to pull himself together. He looks at them one last time and is unable to speak. With his hands he signals: BRAVO, YANKEE.

He walks away with the marine guard.

Eight

THE BUS IS WARM, TOO warm, as buses often are in the winter, and has about it the bus smell of fuel oil and never-aired upholstery. Billy and Mule add the smoke of their cigarettes to the staleness of the bus as they sit in the back seat. Mule takes a newspaper from the empty seat next to him. It is folded in the middle and he flips through it until he finds page one. He reads intently and with some effort for a few minutes, then says to Billy, "This'll tickle you, Billy. Remember that destroyer, the *Hummel*, that got rammed a couple of months ago by that Canadian carrier?"

"Yeah, a shitpotful of crew got deep-sixed. Thirty-some."

"Thirty-eight. Yeah, well, they court-martialed the old man and put the cock to him. Negligent, der'liction of duty and like that."

"What'd he catch?"

"This'll tickle you. Sentenced to a reprimand."

Billy closes his mouth and lets the smoke flow out of his nostrils.

"Was that a full-dress reprimand or a slip-it-to-him-with-Vaseline-on-it reprimand?"

"Paper and verbal both."

"Son-of-a-bitch."

Mule continues to leaf through the paper.

"This dude's a commander, though," he says. "He'll have a hillbilly hell of a time ever making captain. Won't ever have a ship again, for sure."

"I guess it don't make a rat's ass to the thirty-eight on the bottom."

"Well, when you give it some thought, this poor bastard is in bad shape with a reprimand on his record."

"Yeah," says Billy. "It ain't gonna be easy getting a decent table at the officer's club."

Mule rolls the newspaper into a tight shaft and taps his knee with it.

"You're the honcho," he says. "What now?"

"No more," answers Billy.

"You gonna pull some of that der'liction of duty shit on me?"

"Reprimand the hell out of me."

"Anyway, whaddaya wanna do?"

Billy takes a long drag and stuffs the butt into an ashtray.

"Mule, I shoulda let the kid run."

"That's just talk."

"Maybe so, but it's talk that I mean."

"If we could do it over again, we'd do it the same, so what's the good of jiving yourself?"

"Don't you think I know that? That's the whole problem. I'm talking about what we *shoulda* done, man."

"How the hell does anybody know what we shoulda done? We only know what we done, what we were supposed to do."

"But it ain't right.

"What ain't?"

"The whole thing. What we done."

"If we done what we was told to do, then it must be we done right."

"You saw that kid. What's this. What's that. Full of questions, like a child. You wanted to rumple his hair for him, buy him a thick chocolate shake. Not take him to a place like that and leave him with bastards like that who don't even know him or understand him like we do."

"We done what we were told to do."

"Don't we have a mind of our own?"

"Ah, ha," says Mule, "that's the crotch of the whole problem."

Billy lights another cigarette, inhales deeply, and again lets the smoke flow out of his nostrils, with a sigh just audible.

"That kid," he says, "coulda been a good signalman one day. He had a feel for it. All they had to do was take care of that little sickness and they'd have had themselves a good man and a good shipmate. Instead they got shit. What a deal. The kid wasn't ready for it. What a waste. You know, you and me and Larry are three good men, well-trained, you and me at least, and here we are boozing and whoring and pissing around the countryside and taking one of our own to the brig when we should be doing man's work instead."

"It ain't been good, this detail."

Billy turns and looks out the window and says, “Christ, I want a ship. I’m sick of buses and trains and land passing by outside the window, and I’m sick of barrooms and whorehouses, and I’m sick of the smell of piss and smoke and rancid mayonnaise. This ain’t no kind of life for a grown man.”

“Hey, you’re the dude on the recruiting poster in front of the post office. After fourteen years, you saying you found out you don’t like it?”

“I ain’t talking about the navy. I’m talking about *this*. We’re coming to the time when we hafta tally it all up and see what it amounts to, and the thing is, it amounts to *this shitty detail*, Mule. You and me are a string of Polish sausages, forty-nine-cents-a-pound stuff. It took this Portsmouth detail to bring it all home to me.”

“But what’re we gonna *do*, man. We hafta *do* something.”

“You be the honcho for a minute and tell me.”

In the Boston terminal they sit at the lunch counter but neither orders food. They drink bitter black coffee. Mule spins around slowly on his stool for one complete revolution, looking at the terminal around him, and says, “God Almighty, Billy we’re going home again.”

“Home is where you got a locker and a place to lie down.”

“For a quarter you get a locker, to lie down on you get a bench.”

“Be it ever so humble there’s no place like the terminal.”

“’Cept another terminal,” adds Mule.

“Christ, would I like to know what’s happening to me. This is as rotten as I ever felt.”

"Me too," says Mule. "I feel like I been sucking on a goat's hind hoof. It's the kid. I wish he was a wise-ass messcook who coldcocked a commander and went over the hill. I wish he would have big-mouthed about how no goddamn brig was gonna hold him. I wish he was a commie trying to start up trouble. I wish he would have called me a nigger bastard."

"If wishes was dishes you'd own Horn and Hardhart," says Billy.

"Funny," says Mule, "I ain't gonna sit here all night drinking coffee and listening to arrivals and departures."

"You know what I wanted to do, Mule? When we got outside the brig?"

"Huh?"

"I wanted to pick up a rock and throw it at the goddamn place. Stupid, right? Like a damn kid, I wanted to pick up a rock and wing it against a place I didn't like. I thought that if I could knock off one-sixteenth of a square inch of the place, destroy just that much of it, it would be enough for the time being. But I didn't even have the balls to do that."

"Pretty lucky. If you got caught, it'd be your ass, and if you didn't, big deal, you chipped off a piece of Portsmouth."

"It wasn't the size of the chip, it was symbolic."

"Huh?" says Mule.

"If I don't get a lick in here soon, I'm gonna lose my rights to jockey shorts."

Mule laughs and says, "I'm laughing, but I know it ain't so damn funny. I'm feeling the same way."

"You got anything in mind?"

"Not a thing. I wish I did."

"Well, we can spend the night here or go on to New York or Philly or right on back to Shit City if you want to."

"I'd just as soon not do that right this minute," says Mule.

"Well, where *do* you want to go right this minute, 'cause I've had it with this terminal."

"I could go for a beer, with a little something on the side."

They go to a bar and order boilermakers. Mule spins around on his stool and says, "God Almighty, we're home again."

They drink the whiskey and wash it down with the beer. They watch TV for a few minutes before Billy asks, "You ever been married, Mule?"

"Never was. Why buy a cow when milk is so cheap?"

"Well, marriage if it works out is a helluva way for two people to live a life. There's a lot to be said for it. Even if it don't work out, like with Char and me, well, hell, you got the best parts to remember and the rest you forget. You take Char and me, whenever I think about her the thoughts are good ones. She's a good old girl and we had a fine few months together."

"I'm with you so far, partner."

"Now, here's what bothers me. What happens one day when in a marriage the husband says to the wife, after they've been together for years, 'You're a pig.' And he ain't only saying it, he means it and believes it. He just discovered it's true. And what happens when she turns back to him, cool as ice, and says, 'If you wasn't the dumbest Polack in six states you'da known *years* ago I was a pig.'"

"I'm for letting that old married couple worry about their own black asses," says Mule.

"Okay," says Billy, "but that old married couple is me and the Pig Bitch Navy."

"Uh-oh," says Mule.

An hour passes, an hour and a half. Billy spreads his change on the bar in even rows of nickels, dimes, and quarters. He asks the bartender for two dollars' worth of change and adds that to the rows.

"What're you doing?" asks Mule. "Playing war?"

"Nope. Getting out of the navy. Kissing the pig good-bye," says Billy.

"With two dollars in change? Your aunt's ass."

"Mule, I had a fine life with Charlotte. She's a good woman. And, she wants me back."

"Yeah, yeah, yeah."

"Well, she does. Told me so when I went back up. Remember when we were on the street, getting a cab?"

"Yeah, and what are you gonna do on the outside? Go up on the Empire State Building and run up a string of pennants? Nobody pays a signalman on the outside."

"I can pump gas. I can wait tables."

"Your aunt's ass."

"Well, goddamn . . ."

"How long have you been on this hitch?"

"Two years."

"In two years, you'll have only four more for twenty. You'll change your mind."

"Who's to say I have to wait for two years?"

"You're so full of it," says Mule.

"You think so, huh? Well, I'm gonna pick up my two dollars in change, and I'm gonna go into that booth, and I'm gonna call up my *wife*, and I'm gonna leave your ass high and dry in Boston, Massachusetts."

"Hotel Alpha, Hotel Alpha."

"Who's to stop me?"

"Not me, partner," says Mule.

Another half hour passes and Billy asks for another dollar's worth of change. He feels the effect of the beer and whiskey on his empty stomach. His fingers are becoming pleasantly numb as they line up the change on the bar. He stacks the change, picks up the two stacks, and says, "Here I go."

"Yeah, yeah, yeah," chants Mule.

Billy staggers to the phone booth. He gets Charlotte's number from information and tells the operator that he is unable to remember the number or dial the machine. He asks her to please dial the number for him. He can hear the phone ring once. *Char, it's Billy, and I'm here to tell you . . .* The phone rings a second time. *To tell you that . . .* It rings a third time. *That I'm kissing the pig good-bye.* The phone rings a fourth, fifth, sixth, seventh time. There is no answer.

Billy returns to the bar. Mule looks at the expression on his face and says, "If it ain't the newlywed civilian. Do I get to kiss the bride?"

"You know, Mule, after this is all over you and me are going to meet someplace to have one hell of a fight . . . and I hit *hard*."

"In the meantime, in between time.

"You can go your way and I'm going mine."

"I think I'll stick around with you."

"No, you ain't. Go on back to Norfolk like you're supposed to. That's what you were ordered to do."

"I've got a mind of my own, you know."

"No, you don't. Do what you're supposed to."

"I can do what I want to," says Mule.

"No, you can't. Beat it. Give my regards to the ladies."

"Look, goddamn it, let's just cut the shit. You don't give me orders. No one gives me orders 'less I damn well want to follow them. You tried to make me sleep on that damn bed while you slept on the cot, but you couldn't do it, could you? Now you're trying to make me go back to Norfolk while you stay in Boston. Well, you can't do that either. We started this son-of-a-bitching detail together and we are going to wind it up together, and I don't care what a battle wagon full of admirals says about it. I am a man. With a mind of my own."

"You're a mule. And they sure named you the right thing."

They take a cheap hotel room with a cheap TV set and to it they take two bottles of cheap wine. They sit in their skivvies and drink the wine from the bottles and watch TV and look for something even remotely like the life they are living, but they do not see it.

When the wine is gone and they are drunk, they fall into bed and sleep for twelve hours.

Mule awakens first and says to Billy, "I'll flip you to see who gets dressed and gets groceries."

Mule loses the toss and returns with large cardboard containers of coffee and a bag of jelly-filled doughnuts. They eat breakfast and go back to sleep.

When they wake up again the early evening news is on the air. There is an on-the-scene report of a local attempted bank robbery. Two men lie dead on the sidewalk, their feet sticking out from under gray blankets. One of them has lost his shoe. The officers who shot them are being interviewed.

The older of the two officers, and man in charge, is saying, "One of the tellers, uh, set off a silent alarm, and, uh, we received the radio message in our, uh, black and white, and proceeded to the scene. We observed two Caucasian males, uh, leaving the scene carrying brown paper bags and what appeared to be, uh, guns. Officer Breslin and I took cover behind our, uh, black and white, and ordered the suspects to, uh, halt."

"Did they heed your orders?" prompts the reporter.

"Uh, no sir, they did not. They made movements for their guns and continued to run. Officer Breslin and I drew our, uh, service revolvers and fired off two rounds apiece."

"Where were the suspects hit?" asks the reporter.

"I, uh, understand that Officer Breslin's suspect was hit in the back of the neck. Mine was, I understand, uh, hit two times in the, uh, head."

"Was all of the stolen money recovered?" asks the reporter.

"I understand that they're counting it now, uh, but it is assumed that all the, uh, money was recovered."

"Thank you Officers Mundy and Breslin. This is Ed White at the scene of the attempted robbery."

Billy says, "Dammit, why am I always for the bad guys, the shits of the world who'd probably sell their mothers for a beer? Why can't *I* be part of the decent world? Who the hell *are* the decent people of the world? Tell me, Mule, so I can be for *them* for a change."

"Ain't that a kick in the ass?"

The report is followed by two commercials, back to back. Three jubilant women declare that they're glad they put borax in Fab because everything comes out whiter now, even bloodstains. It's clear a major milestone in their lives has been reached.

The second commercial shows two men and a woman, individually, describing their particular kinds of headaches and the speed with which Excedrin clears them up.

"There they are," says Mule, "the decent people of the world. You asked for it."

"How can I be for *them?*" says Billy. "We ain't gonna make it, Mule. We've got liberty, and we're dying up here, and Larry is getting his lumps in Portsmouth, and those pricks are worrying about their stupid damn clothes coming out *white* and their little headaches going away. You and me, we ain't gonna make it."

Billy rises to his knees in bed and screams at the set, "Take your white tornado, take your two mints in one, take your goddamn cigarette that both of you can smoke, and *fuck all that shit*! We're *dying* up here, you bastards!"

He collapses on his face and puts his hands on the back of his head.

"Flip you to see who gets the wine," says Mule.

Billy lifts his right hand and waves it in a go-away gesture. "Okay," says Mule, "but next time, dammit, you're going."

They live this way for days, on wine and cigarettes, coffee and doughnuts, sleep and TV.

One day when Walter Cronkite ends his report with, "That's the way it is . . ." Mule says, "The way it is, Billy, is we're AWOL, as of today if my reckoning is right. Ain't it funny the way you slip into things?"

"Or outa them."

"Yeah."

"First time for me," says Billy.

"Me too," says Mule.

"It ain't the worst thing that could happen."

"No, probably just the beginning of the worst thing."

"There are buses, trains, and planes," says Billy.

"Well, do you wanna take one and we can dream up a line of shit?"

"Not just yet. You?"

"Hell, if I leave, you'll just get yourself in a mess of trouble. Besides, we're partners and I kinda like you. You're a good . . ."

"What?"

"I was gonna say you're a good nigger. That's member talk. But dammit, you *are* a good nigger."

"Hope so. Try to be anyway." Billy pulls himself up to a sitting position. "Old buddy, what do you think about us going outdoors and getting the stink blown off us?"

"Technically, you know, we're wanted men."

"That's nice. That's a real nice way to put it, you know? With so many unwanted men around, I don't mind."

They shave and put on their uniforms. On the dresser lie their .45's and SP arm bands.

"Do you see us having any more use for these little bastards?" asks Billy.

"Don't suppose."

Billy lays the .45 in the palm of his hand and slowly moves his hand up and down.

"What're you doing?" asks Mule.

"Hefting the weight of it. It ain't as heavy as it looks."

"What're you thinking?"

"Let's put 'em in my AWOL bag and make a deal with a friendly pawnbroker. Should be worth fifty bucks apiece."

Mule groans softly. "You are one *badass*. Selling navy issue arms!"

"Keep yours if you want to."

"What for? I can be as bad an ass as you are."

"Let's throw the handcuffs in too."

"Oh, sure, what the hell."

They lock the door behind them and walk down the narrow dusty corridor. "Mule?"

"Huh?"

"You're one good Polack."

JERDAN'S

WE BUY * SELL * TRADE EVERYTHING

There are pigeon droppings on the tattered awning that flaps in the breeze. On the other side of the streaked windows, music: guitars, trombones, drums, trumpets. Fun: roller skates, jewelry, cameras. Work: power tools, typewriters.

They pull the collars of their peacoats around their necks and look at the wares.

"Okay," says Billy. "What's our rock-bottom price?"

"Hell, I don't know."

"Well, what's a .45 worth?"

"That depends on whether you're buying or selling, or the United States Navy."

"Look, is this a big deal to you?"

"I didn't say a goddamn word."

"I want to tell you right now, so we understand each other. I am beyond it, man. So with me there's no worry, no fear, there's only me beyond it. Just so we understand each other."

"That clears the whole thing up like nobody's business, Billy. Thanks a shitpotful."

"Okay, so what are we asking?"

"Fifty apiece, like you said."

"That's probably too high."

"Thirty then, what's the difference? A bag of peanuts for Chrissake. I don't care."

Billy goes inside, walks around the stack of lockers and luggage in the center of the aisle and approaches the pawnbroker, who watches Billy carefully but says nothing.

"Hyuh," says Billy.

The pawnbroker nods.

"Got a little thing or two here I'd like to sell you outright."

Still nothing from the pawnbroker. Billy zips open the bag and produces one of the guns. He puts it on the counter and slides it across with the back of his hand. The pawnbroker lifts a corner of his lip enough for Billy to notice the reaction. He does not touch the gun.

"Where'd you get it, son?"

"You can have it cheap. Thirty dollars."

He picks it up and turns it around in his hands.

"Where'd you get it?"

"Look, I want to sell it. Thirty bucks."

The pawnbroker slides it back across the counter.

"Not here."

Billy puts it back into the bag and leaves. "No sale," he says to Mule.

They walk past the paperback book arcade and the all-night movie, three features for sixty cents, to

HAROLD'S
MONEY TO LOAN
LOW INTEREST RATES, EST. 1925

In the window are many knives made to look like switchblades, but without the rapid release mechanism that makes them illegal.

They are all open, the blades stuck into a cardboard box, suggesting the conclusion of some unspeakable ritual. Billy goes inside and in a few moments is on the street again, in time to see a wino press a crusty index finger against one nostril and blow, voiding the other of eight inches of snot.

"How'd we do?" asks Mule.

"Nobody wants to touch these damn pieces, like they had the clap or something. Sold the handcuffs, though."

"For what?"

"Two bucks."

"Last of the big wheeler-dealers, ain't you, Billy."

"What's three into two?"

"Too tough for me. Why?"

"A third of this is Larry's plus a third of what we get for the pieces."

REGENCY LOAN & JEWELRY CO.
MONEY TO LOAN
GUNS & AMMO

Nothing.

-ROXY-
MONEY ON EVERYTHING
WE BUY ANYTHING OF VALUE

They both go inside this time and show the .45 to the pawnbroker. He examines it and gives it back to them.

"I never saw this," he says. "If I saw a gun stamped US Government, I would call the F.B.I. Any pawnbroker would."

Billy drops the gun into the AWOL bag and zips the bag as they hurry out of the shop. On the street they slow each other down and try to look casual, turning now and again to look over their shoulders. A bus stops at the corner. They run to it and board it. Billy puts the bag under his seat, and together they look out of the window for G-man types.

"The F.B.I.," says Mule. "Lordy, Lordy."

They ride twelve blocks, get off, and slip into the nearest bar, where they feel hidden, but still not entirely safe. They drink their beers. Billy holds the AWOL bag on his lap.

Mule says, "That does it. The goddamn F.B.I. We're goners."

"Hell, Boston is full of sailors."

"Yeah, but how many of them are salt and pepper, toting two .45's in an AWOL bag?"

Mule slaps the bag on Billy's lap.

"Let me think a minute," says Billy.

Mule keeps quiet and looks at the signs behind the bar: *We don't take checks any more. We have a good supply left over from last year. This is a non-profit organization. We didn't plan it that way. It just worked out that way.*

"Well?" Mule finally asks.

Billy is looking in the wall mirror behind the bar.

"Have you noticed my nose lately?" he asks.

"Here, lemme see."

Billy swivels around on his stool.

"Nothing wrong with it," says Mule.

"It's getting bigger."

"You're about a crazy bastard."

"I ain't kidding you. It's getting bigger. I should be able to tell about my own nose."

Mule looks at it a second time. "I just remembered something," he says. "I heard once someplace that when you get older your body shrinks, you know, like if you're six foot tall you wind up only five-ten. Yessir, that's a scientific fact. I've seen lots of old people who were bigger when they were young people. But here's the thing—your whole body shrinks but for one part—your nose. That's why it looks bigger. It ain't growing, the rest of you is shrinking. You're getting old, Billy Bad-Ass."

"This detail sure cut off a couple of years at the other end, boy, I tell you that."

"So, here I am with a twelve-inch prick and a bucket full of balls and he *still* calls me boy."

Billy pays no attention to him. He holds his nose between his fingers, gauging its size. He gives the impression that any decision made will be directly related to the condition of his nose.

Finally he says, "Okay drink up. I got an idea."

They go outside and walk to the mailbox at the corner. Billy casually turns 360 degrees. When he is sure he isn't being noticed, he takes the two .45's, with guard belts and holsters, and drops the whole business into the mailbox.

"Special delivery, sealed with a kiss," he says.

Mule puts his head between his arms on the mailbox and laughs or cries, it is hard to say which.

They go back to their room and sleep the sleep of the newly unburdened. The next evening the tag item on the news broadcast is a funny little story about two government pistols being found in a local mailbox. The F.B.I. is investigating the matter.

The bar has behind it those electric signs that all but the poorest bars have. Cold blue water cascading down a fall, suggesting an experience comparable to drinking a bottle of their beer; duck hunters, good fellows all, in a blind with a V of wild birds appearing in the upper left corner; a large bottle of liquid solution in which gambol globs of hot wax.

The bartender is old and fat, and he smells bad, but only if he leans over the bar in a posture of intimacy. Otherwise, the smell of the place is a stand-off between urine and disinfectant. The bartender leans back in a barber's chair he has had installed behind the bar and from that position keeps an eye on the progress of his drinkers. He slouches down in the chair, both feet against the footrest. From time to time he reaches to the bar and grabs a small pretzel from a bowl and pops it into his mouth.

Billy and Mule order shots and beers. Mule throws his shot down, pauses for a minute until he feels a slight deadening of his lips, and then revives them with a swallow of cold draft beer. Billy saves the shot and sips his beer as he watches a three-way dart contest taking place in the corner of the room. The dartboard is attached to the wall, surrounded by its black scoring board. Extending over the top of it is a gooseneck lamp, the shield of which has multiple punctures from wayward darts.

They are playing triple-thirteen, low man buys the beers. Before the shooter may shoot the inning, he must first shoot three darts at the thirteenth inning and score a triple. Should he shoot two triples on thirteen, his subsequent score for the inning would be doubled. Billy watches the game closely. It is seldom that one of the shooters scores a triple-thirteen.

Billy swivels around to Mule, who is on his second boilermaker, and whispers, "How much money you got?"

Mule reaches into his jumper pocket, counts his cash, and says, "Fourteen, plus the change on the bar."

"Gimme the fourteen. I'm gonna hustle us a dart game."

"Up yours," says Mule.

Billy empties his pocket and counts sixteen dollars plus change. "Look, we got thirty bucks between us. That ain't gonna last the night. Then where the hell are we?"

"Who the hell cares?"

"You can look at it that way if you want to, but I'll tell you something, I know how to shoot darts. Every bar in Schuylkill County has a dartboard and I was hitting those bars before I was sixteen. I don't want to brag, Mule, but I never lost a dime on the board. I can win us a nice little grubstake here."

"Okay, take the damn money. It ain't like it was a big thing."

Billy stuffs the thirty dollars into his jumper pocket and takes his beer to the end of the bar, next to the shooters.

"Is this a game that only three can play?"

"You wouldn't try to be hustling us, would you, sailor?" says one of them.

"Whaddaya mean?"

"I've had guys before come up and say, 'How do you play this game?' and then wind up walking away talking to myself."

"Oh, I played before," says Billy. "I just meant would you take a fourth in to play."

"This is a friendly game, low man pays for the beers."

"Sure. I'm a friendly sailor," says Billy.

They play two games and Billy comes in last each time, but not by much. He buys them their beers and kids with them and says he's only warming up. One of them says, "How 'bout we play a buck a man. I'm getting a sour stomach from all this beer."

"I told you, man, I'm only warming up. I don't wanna take your money," says Billy.

Another one says, "Well, around this time a night we usually play for money anyway. You can drop out if you want to."

They shoot another game and Billy comes in a poor second. He must pay a dollar to the winner. From his end of the bar, Mule says, "I thought you knew how to play this game," and knocks back Billy's shot of whiskey.

"Hellfire, I gotta warm up, that's all," says Billy.

"Look," says the man who just won, "what about we shoot one more game, five bucks a man and that'll be it for the night. Okay?"

"Five bucks," says one of the others. He has never played for such high stakes.

"One game only?" asks the third.

"Hell, I'll shoot. It's only money," says Billy.

They each shoot one dart at the bull's-eye. Billy is closest and calls the game. "Five or better, five innings."

In the first inning Billy is the only one to score five. No one scores in the second or third. In the fourth inning two other players score five for a three-way tie. In the final inning one of Billy's two opponents fails to score, but the other shoots a five. When Billy puts his toe at the line of nails hammered into the floor to indicate the shooter's line he must shoot a five to tie, six to win. His first dart hits the red for two points. His second dart does likewise. With his third he can shoot for the easy tie and send it to the next inning or he can try for the harder two-pointer. He snaps his wrist and sends the dart kissing off the other two for a three-pointer.

"Now that's more like it," says Mule.

"I think I've been hustled again," says the first man.

They pay Billy a total of fifteen. The one who proposed the five-dollar game wants to continue, but his two friends will not risk their money. Billy shoots him man-to-man for three straight wins and collects another fifteen.

At the end of the third match, another customer comes into the bar and the three dart-shooters brighten.

"Hi, Vinnie, how they hanging? Have a beer on me."

The one who has just lost to Billy says, "Vinnie, will you play this Popeye? He's been kicking the shit outa all of us."

"You a hustler, sailor?" asks Vinnie.

"Good shooter is all," says Billy.

"Good enough for some competition?"

"The board is always open to a challenge."

From his barber's chair, the bartender says to Mule, "Tell your friend to take his money and run. Vinnie's a money shooter, best in the neighborhood."

"Well, hell," says Billy, "I'm not exactly an amputee, you know."

"How much do you want to shoot for, sailor?" asks Vinnie.

Billy spreads his money on the bar.

"I got fifty-seven bucks here says I can beat you one outa one, winner takes all."

"You're on," says Vinnie and counts out his fifty-seven dollars onto the bar.

The other customers move their stools closer to the board for a good view of a big money game. Even the bartender gets out of his barber chair and leans over the bar.

Mule says, "Bartender, how's my credit?"

But the bartender does not bother to answer such a foolish question.

Billy shoots at the cork for game and position. The dart lands against the wire, on the outside. Vinnie's lands dead center. "Seven, no count, three innings."

"You're shitting me," says Billy.

"Shoot," says Vinnie.

Billy shoots three straight darts into the red eye for a total of six points, not enough for a count. Vinnie sends his first two into the triple space and shoots an easy single for a score.

Mule nudges one of the customers and says, "Hey, buddy, got any spare change?" The customer ignores him.

On the second inning Billy shoots two straight triples and follows them with a rather shaky dart in the red for a total of eight. Vinnie follows with a casual seven points. Fourteen to eight.

In the third inning, Billy shoots a triple and then quickly before he gets nervous, sends two right under the first dart for a total of seven, a score. Fifteen to fourteen, Billy's favor.

In the bottom of the third inning, Vinnie shoots two close together in the red in the hope of sending the third dart right above them for a score. He pauses for a long moment at the shooting line. Mule whispers to no one in particular, "Jesus Christ, I'm messing my skivvies."

Billy turns his back on the shooter and swallows his beer. Vinnie's delivery is not smooth. The dart glances upward off the other two and goes into the blue at an angle. Four points, no score.

There is a hubbub of excitement in the bar and the customers immediately begin a shot-by-shot rehash of the game. Billy gives one stack of fifty-seven dollars to Mule and grips the other stack in his fist.

"Give 'em all a beer," he says to the bartender "and take one for yourownself."

Vinnie gulps down his beer and says, "You're a damn good shooter, sailor."

"Told you I was."

"Yeah." Vinnie puts on his coat and leaves.

The customers drink their beers to Billy's health and he answers with a gracious tilt of his own glass.

"You know what we should do with some of this dough?" says Billy.

"Get drunk," Mule answers.

"Yeah, naturally, but what we should also do is send some of it to Larry."

"You figure he got any use for bread there?"

"He's gotta have cigarettes and shaving cream and stuff. Maybe they have a gedunk there where he can get some candy, I don't know. Besides, we're partners."

"You know, Billy, sometimes you're a real human being, I mean that."

"How much do you think we should send?"

"Christ, ten dollars should last forever in the brig."

"Let's send him twenty."

"Goddamn, let's send the kid thirty, if it comes to that."

Mule peels off fifteen dollars from his roll and Billy matches it. "Bartender, you got a piece of paper and a pen and maybe an envelope?" asks Billy.

"Do I look like a damn P. O.?"

"Well son-of-a-bitch, I'm *gonna* leave you a big tip."

"I think in a drawer here I got."

The bartender rummages through a drawer and gives Billy the material.

"You wanna write the letter?" Billy asks Mule.

"Hell, no, I'm terrible at that. You write it. Just say hi for me."

Billy smooths out the paper in front of him, moves his glass of beer out of the way, and shakes his pen hand a few times in preparation for the miraculous act of writing.

Mule says, "Whaddaya gonna make, a Twentieth-Century-fucking-Fox production outa this?"

"I gotch your production, partner—swinging. I'll have you know I was told by very good authority on the subject that I coulda been a writer of skin books. You gotta get in the mood for writing something, you know."

"You're only sending coin to Larry in the brig, you ain't writing a noble prize."

"It's Nobel, fartferbrains, and you don't write the prize, you write the book that wins the prize."

"Well, pardon my goddamn ignorance, my old man wasn't a teacher."

"Yeah, I know, he was a rabbit runaway."

"You trying to start something?"

"Why the hell are you being so miserable all of a sudden?"

"Me? You're the one with the goddamn grasshopper up his ass."

"Well, son-of-a-bitch you can shag ass, you know."

"Well, son-of-a-bitch if I won't."

Mule picks up his money and puts on his peacoat.

"If you have any call for me I'll be across the goddamn street in my own gin mill."

"Well, fuck you and fuck a whole bunch of gin mills."

"Well, fuck you and I hope you die with a hard-on."

"Yeah, well if I do, it'll be up your girl's wing wang at the time."

"Piss around a pretzel!" yells Mule and slams the door behind him.
"A friendly disagreement?" asks the bartender.
"Yeah," says Billy.
To himself he says, as he writes:

Dear Larry,

Bet you're surprised to hear from us. How are they treating you? Since you've seen the green stuff falling out of the envelope, I might as well get to the point. Old Mule and I came on what you might call a windfall—strictly legit, of course. We wanted to cut you in. We took a real shine to you, kid, and think of you as our good friend, and hope that the feeling is mutual. Like you said, we were only doing our job. Another detail. But you and I know it isn't as simple as that. Believe me, Larry, if Mule and I could split the 8 with you, we'd be willing in a minute to do 2 and 3/4 or whatever the hell it comes out as. But we could never let you go. Just couldn't. Okay, if it boils down to your ass or our ass, well then that's what it boils down to. I hope you'll never come to a day when you hate us for it. Oh, by the way, Mules says hi. He's still an old kick in the ass. Hope you can use the loot. If they open your mail and take it, let me know. Don't know what I could do about it, though.

Pals and shipmates,
Billy Bad-Ass and Mule Mulhall

Billy reads the letter and crosses out the last two sentences. If Larry doesn't get the letter he won't be able to let him know he didn't. He folds the letter around the bills and seals the envelope. He addresses it to:

Larry Meadows, SN
Portsmouth Naval Prison
Portsmouth, N.H.

"Hey, Sal the Barber, you got a stamp?"

"I don't got a stamp. I gave you a pen 'n paper 'n envelope. Now you want a stamp, next it'll be running to the box with it. Piss on it."

"You don't have to bite off my head. I only wanted a lousy six-cent stamp. Remember your tip."

"I don't got no stamp anyway."

Billy puts the envelope into his inside peacoat pocket and taps the pocket with his hand. He orders another boilermaker and again thinks of Charlotte. In four hours he could be with her. It would be as simple as boarding a train, an activity at which Billy is an expert. She would want him to be there. Chances are she would even hide him from the F.B.I., the navy, and whatever other institutions are interested in cases like his.

Yet he finds it impossible to get up and go to New York, and he doesn't know why. He doesn't especially like Boston, but he doesn't see how he can get up and leave. He hopes that at closing time he will be able at least to get up and leave this bar.

In the morning Billy wakes up in a fit of smoker's cough. He holds the edge of the dresser and leans forward, doubling farther over with each spasm.

"You're coughin' a lot better this morning," says Mule.

"Fuck off," gasps Billy.

"Have a cigarette. Die of cancer. I almost give a cow's crap."

"I don't sweat dying of cancer. They won't give me the chance to."

"Who won't?" asks Mule.

Billy motions with his head toward the window.

"They won't," he says.

They live in their room that day on wine and potato chips. The next day they venture out for a hamburger and on the following day they go outside for a bowl of vegetable soup, which, unlike the hamburger, manages to stay down.

They eventually return to the scene of Billy's success. The dart shooters laugh good-naturedly when they see him and say that they won't be fished into a match with him, but Billy feels too bad to shoot anyhow.

The bartender gives them their boilermakers and says, "What can we do for you today? Envelopes, pencils, stamps?"

Billy remembers the letter to Larry. It is still in his pocket.

"I forgot to get a stamp for Larry's money," he says.

"That's bright," says Mule.

"Well, you know, dammit, you don't have no light-duty chit. Why didn't you trot on down to the post office and get a damn stamp?"

"'Cause I was scared I'd see your ugly fucking picture on the wall."

"If you feel that way, dammit, you don't have to park your ugly fat ass on the stool next to mine."

"Fucking-ay-John Ditty-Bag-well-told I don't. I'm going to my own gin mill across the damn street."

"I gotch your gin mill."

Mule holds up three fingers in a Boy Scout salute and says, "Read between the lines."

"Yeah, I see your I.Q."

"No, man, your number of friends."

Mule slams the door behind him and storms over to his own gin mill.

"Glad to see you two made up," says the bartender.

"Since you offered, I could use another piece of paper and an envelope and a pencil."

The bartender gets them and says, "This keeps up, I'm gonna charge tuition here."

Billy finds it hard to believe that he has one letter in his pocket, ready for mailing, and is about to write a second. He is not used to writing so many letters in a short time.

Dear Charlotte,

You remember I told you I had a lot of thinking to do. Well, I'm still doing it. You probably thought we just went right on by N. Y. to Norfolk, but the fact is we're still up here in Boston. Thinking, like I told you. Well, to be honest with you, Char, there's been an awful lot of drinking and awful little thinking. The booze must have wore down my brain cells because I haven't been able to string two thoughts together ever since we left Larry at the brig. Things have just happened by themselves since then. All I know is I sure as hell ain't the sailor I used to be. My brain gets that far and quits on me. As far as the other thing that

I talked to you about, we'll just have to hang loose and find out where I'm going.

Love,
Billy

He folds it, puts it into an envelope, and addresses it to Charlotte. It joins Larry's letter in the inside peacoat pocket.

"How 'bout one more of these bartender. I'm gonna have just one more drink, and then I'm gonna have another."

He runs his dirty hand through his hair, in a furtive search for something he thinks may be living there.

His right hand flat on the bar, Billy sits with his face against his hand, his left hand also on the bar next to his dirty, misshapen white hat. There are some random razor swaths on a face of stubble. His hair is coming to resemble the wild head of brown hair his grandfather, the cabinetmaker, wore. His fingernails are nibbled to the quick, and some of his cuticles are inflamed. His eyes are closed.

He is ignored by the bartender. The last shot and a beer he served Billy is still untouched. Of the other customers, three old men and an old woman, only the woman has commented on him, saying it was disgraceful that an American fighting man should look so foul and nasty.

A second class quartermaster and a third class storekeeper on Shore Patrol duty stop at the window and peer through the streaked glass. They come inside and the second class taps Billy on the shoulder. There is no response. Now he takes him by both shoulders and gives him a firm shake. Billy's head wobbles from side to side and he mumbles incoherently.

The second class turns him around on his seat and says, "Let's have your I.D."

Billy fumbles for his wallet and hands it to him. He turns back to the bar.

"Chrissake," say the second class, "William Buddusky, huh? We have the skinny on you. You look like shit, Buddusky, if you don't mind my saying so."

"Quite all right old man," says Billy in a mock British accent.

"You and your pal the dudes who dropped the pieces in the mailbox, right?" The SP chuckles. "Everybody on the base is talking about you birds."

"A legend in my own time, yakety, yakety, yak, yak, yak."

"I'd give my right nut to sit in on your court-martial."

"Well, let's have it and I'll drop it in my goddamn beer here."

"That's gonna be some court-martial."

"Fuck you and fuck a whole bunch of court-martials."

"Okay, where's your partner Mulhall?" he asks to Billy's back.

"In the joint across the street," answers Billy.

"What's he doing there?"

"The usual thing—dropping pennies in the pisser, making wishes."

"Let's pack up and go get him. You guys have had it."

"After I finish my drink," says Billy.

"Now!" says the second class and prods Billy with his club.

Billy throws down the shot, lifts the beer chaser between his forefinger and thumb and drains the glass before he takes it from his lips. He puts the glass back on the bar and says, "After I finish my drink."

Billy staggers between the two of them to the bar across the street. Mule is in front of the jukebox, trying to read the selections available. He rocks back and forth on his feet, not in time to the music playing. Billy is left near the door in the custody of the third class. The other approaches Mule and says, "Party's over, Mulhall, time to pay for the tab."

"Mulhall? You're confusing me with another nigger by the same name."

"So show me an I.D."

"What you're saying is I've been captured."

"Hope to shit," says the SP.

"Looks like an inside job to me."

"Pack 'em up."

Mule says nothing. He walks toward the door. The second class picks up Mule's white hat from the bar and drops it on his head.

"We got a wagon just down the street," he says.

"*Oh, they brought Bill home in a hurryup wagon, this morning, this evening, so soon,*" Mule sings.

"I remember that song," says Billy. "Carl Sandburg wrote that song. Think so, anyway. Sure wasn't Robert Frost."

They go down the street, Mule and Billy staggering slightly in front, the two SP's walking patiently behind. Mule inclines his head toward Billy and whispers, "You finked on me, didn't you, Billy?"

"Sure. They had us, what the hell."

"They had *you*," says Mule. "I'm harder to capture than that, candy-ass."

A few moments later, Mule says, "I'll let you make it up to me. On the count of three, you get your man and I'll coldcock mine."

He does not give Billy time to think about it or to object. He begins his count: "One, two, *three*!"

Billy spins around and brings a punch right from the ground. It catches the second class on the mouth and nose and lifts him a good six inches from the sidewalk before he goes flat on his back and lies there motionless, his white hat some three feet beyond him.

Mule is convulsed with laughter. He leans against a building and holds his sides as he roars. Billy does not know what to do and simply stands there defenseless as the third class SP gives him two quick knocks on the head with his baton, one on top of the head, one across the temple. Billy's knees buckle, come straight again, and he falls on his face. A trickle of blood runs along his cheek and the sidewalk.

Still laughing, Mule grabs the second class under the armpits and drags him down the street to the paddy wagon.

"Oh, here I come, here I come, my sorry second class in my hand."

The third class cannot help himself. As he watches Mule he too begins to laugh. Their laughter ricochets off the building. The third class grabs Billy under the armpits and drags him behind Mule and the second class to the waiting wagon.

The driver jumps out and says, "What in the huckleberry hell is all this about?"

The third class stops his laughing and says, "Well, we picked us up a helluva billy bad-ass here."

The driver bends over Billy and puts two fingers on his neck. He puts his ear to Billy's heart. He looks up to the other two.

"You picked him up awful hard. Comedy's over. This bad-ass is dead."

Nine

In Boston, in the warm transient barracks, two men sit on opposite sides of a piece of plywood, placed between two bottom bunks to make a table. They are in dungarees, too faded to make out the names stenciled above their left breast pockets. On the plywood between them is a cribbage board, two cups of coffee, half full, the coffee stains running over the edge and down the concave sides. Two hands have been turned over and counted and one of the players is now counting the crib.

"Fifteen-two, fifteen-four, pair is six, and a pair is eight. That little old pussy is gonna lose you this game."

"Ain't over till the last hole's been pegged."

A messenger from the MAA's office, seaman apprentice, opens the door to the transient barracks and fills it with a stab of cold air.

"Shut the fucking hatch, piss head!"

The messenger closes the door and pushes against it with his back until it clicks shut. He blows into his cupped hands and then puts them over his cold ears, and approaches the two players in half steps, making a display of his suffering the cold in order to accomplish his mission and bring joy to one of them and hold on to his job so he won't have to messcook it all day and night in the galley.

"Hi," he says.

They do not answer. One of the players shuffles the cards. The other fingers his cards as they are dealt him.

"One of you named, Wolfe?" asks the messenger. "Waitin' for the *Wilson*?"

"Yeah," says the elder of the two. "She in?"

"No, she ain't due for another ten days."

"So whaddaya want?" asks Wolfe.

The messenger smiles. "You're some kinda lucky bastard," now with an edge.

"Yeah?"

"Yeah. You pulled some good temporary duty."

"I got some good temporary duty. You're looking at it," says Wolfe gesturing toward the table.

"I'm talking about comrats, per diem, on your own kinda temporary duty. The MAA wants to see you right away."

Wolfe makes a move to rise, then says to the messenger, "You got a pencil?"

The messenger puts a hand into his peacoat and pulls one out. Wolfe draws a line next to the last hole he's pegged on the cribbage board. He draws another line next to his opponent's last peg.

"What duty did he pull?" asks the other player.

"Are you ready for this? A funeral detail. Wolfe is gonna escort a stiff home."

"Where?" asks Wolfe.

"Little town in P.A., Andoshen. But that's something, ain't it?"

Wolfe smiles and says, "I'll be damned. I am one lucky bastard. They probably never seen a sailor in uniform there."

"Son-of-a-bitch, why don't I ever pull a benie like that?" says the other.

"I've saved the best part for last," says the messenger and grins.

"All right, lay it on me," says Wolfe, also grinning.

"You got a weed?" asks the messenger.

Wolfe gives him one and lights it for him.

"So what's the best part?" he asks, still grinning.

"The stiff is Billy Bad-Ass," says the messenger. "You know, Billy Bad-Ass."

Wolfe's face freezes for a second in mid-expression.

Epilogue

AIN'T IT FUNNY THE WAY things work out? You draw one shit detail and then you draw another until you draw the last detail. You take static from some "officer and gentleman" who has one hand in the till and the other up his ass, while the poor jerk from Camden you take up the river to the Crossbars Hotel. Then you get drunk, you don't know why, get AWOL, get captured, and jive your partner to tag a Shore Patrol dude on the snot-locker, which happens to break it. You watch while your partner gets the stick laid upalongside the head. It ain't the kinda hurt that kills. But this one does.

So you're issued dungarees with the P stenciled on them, and your white hat is pulled down over your head, you march heel-to-toe, asshole-to-belly button, yelling, "Gangway—prisoner! Gangway—prisoner! Gangway—prisoner!"

I'm like Billy. Give me a ship, any ship. I know what I'm supposed to do there. Would match myself against anybody on the crew. But, the rest of this shit, frankly, I don't understand.

Tomorrow is Sunday and at reveille some will relieve the watch and some will go on holiday routine, but I'm nailed for three years for going over the hill, and "selling or otherwise illegally disposing of government property," and for telling Billy to coldcock an SP and contributing to what they like to call, "Justified Homicide."

Three years bad time. I hope that will be the end of the bad time, but at the bottom of it, I could care less, if I cared at all, which I don't, because I can't help thinking about Billy the Bad-Ass, what a good nigger, and that kid Meadows and his eight years for a lousy forty fucking bananas. I don't ever think about that lieutenant and his redheaded whore in their beer parlor in Portland. What the hell.

About the Author

Darryl Ponicsán divides his time between the Northern California wine country and the Southern California desert. The author of thirteen novels, he has also written several produced screenplays. *The Last Detail,* originally published in 1970, was his first novel, and the movie adapted from it has become a film classic. Most recently, he has completed *Last Flag Flying,* the long-awaited sequel to *The Last Detail,* which has also been adapted into a major movie.